Welcome to…

The Hollywood Hills Clinic

*Where doctors to the stars
work miracles by day—
and explore their hearts' desires by night…*

When hotshot doc James Rothsberg started
the clinic six years ago he dreamed of a
world-class facility, catering to Hollywood's
biggest celebrities, and his team are unrivalled
in their fields. Now, as the glare of the
media spotlight grows, the Hollywood Hills
Clinic is teaming up with the pro-bono
Bright Hope Clinic, and James is reunited
with Dr Mila Brightman…
the woman he jilted at the altar!

When it comes to juggling the care of
Hollywood A-listers with care for the
underprivileged kids of LA *anything* can
happen…and sizzling passions run high in the
shadow of the red carpet. With everything at
stake for James, Mila and the Hollywood Hills
Clinic medical team their biggest challenges
have only just begun!

Find out what happens in the dazzling

The Hollywood Hills Clinic miniseries

Available from April 2016!

Dear Reader,

This is my second involvement in an eight-book series, and while in some ways it's much, much harder than writing solo in other ways it's so much fun. Writing is normally such a solitary occupation—a bit like being an only child—whereas being part of a series is like being part of a large family. Not only do the other authors become my family, but our characters develop and grow together on the pages and form relationships that carry across all the stories.

I cannot wait to read the completed series and revisit my characters to see if they have managed to keep hold of their HEA :)

I really hope you enjoy a taste of LA glamour!

Happy reading,

Emily

FALLING FOR THE SINGLE DAD

BY
EMILY FORBES

Published in Great Britain 2016
By Mills & Boon, an imprint of HarperCollins*Publishers*
1 London Bridge Street, London, SE1 9GF

© 2016 Harlequin Books S.A.

*Special thanks and acknowledgement are given to Emily Forbes
for her contribution to* The Hollywood Hills Clinic *series.*

ISBN: 978-0-263-26405-0

Printed and bound in Great Britain
by CPI Antony Rowe, Chippenham, Wiltshire

Emily Forbes is an award-winning author of Medical Romances for Mills & Boon. She has written over 25 books and has twice been a finalist in the Australian Romantic Book of the Year Award, which she won in 2013 for her novel *Sydney Harbour Hospital: Bella's Wishlist*. You can get in touch with Emily at emilyforbes@internode.on.net or visit her website at emily-forbesauthor.com.

Books by Emily Forbes

Mills & Boon Medical Romance

Tempted & Tamed!

A Doctor by Day...
Tamed by the Renegade

Dr Drop-Dead Gorgeous
Navy Officer to Family Man
Breaking Her No-Dates Rule
Georgie's Big Greek Wedding?
Sydney Harbour Hospital: Bella's Wishlist
Breaking the Playboy's Rules
Daring to Date Dr Celebrity
The Honourable Army Doc
A Kiss to Melt Her Heart
His Little Christmas Miracle
A Love Against All Odds

Visit the Author Profile page at millsandboon.co.uk for more titles.

For Amanda, Ali and Sarah.

Thank you all for an amazing thirty-plus years of friendship. Together we somehow survived our teenage years, the fashions of the eighties, cross-country moves, marriages, babies and now our own teenagers! As we begin to celebrate another round of milestone birthdays I've been thinking about the incredible memories we've created along the way and how lucky I am to have such 'old' friends.

With love xx

CHAPTER ONE

THE HOLLYWOOD SIGN flashed intermittently into Abi's peripheral vision as she wound her way up into the Hollywood Hills. Her heart rate accelerated as she drew closer to her destination and she felt her palms go clammy as her nervousness increased a notch or two. She tightened her grip on the steering wheel, not wanting her hands to slip as she fought back the wave of panic that threatened to overwhelm her. She hadn't expected to feel quite so terrified today. She'd rehearsed this, she'd prepared for this. She could do this.

She had debated about catching a cab for her first day but had decided that if she could drum up the courage to drive that would give her the freedom that waiting for a taxi wouldn't, and in order to prepare she'd done a trial run yesterday with Jonty. She'd needed to know where she was going and she'd needed to make sure it was safe. Bringing Jonty yesterday had given her courage and confidence but today she was travelling solo.

One more corner to go and then she was able to turn off the steep, winding road into the staff parking area for The Hollywood Hills Clinic. The iconic Hollywood sign loomed large above her again, its fresh white paint stark against the dull green and brown of the hillside and the shrubby flora that sprouted there. She swiped her card at the gate and waited nervously for it to open. The staff car park was secure, fenced and gated, and she was relieved to see the addition of good lighting and CCTV cameras. She breathed a sigh of relief as she squeezed her second-hand, two-door, soft-top 4x4 between two immaculately shiny sports cars.

She took a moment to sit quietly in her car as she summoned up the nerve to get out of the vehicle. It had taken all her courage to get into her car this morning and now that she was here she needed to find some more. Starting a new job and meeting new colleagues was going to test her limits. She was in the rebuilding phase, trying to cope with the stress of life, and anything unexpected could, and often still did, unsettle her. She needed to find the strength to get out of her car. She closed her eyes and rehearsed the process her psychologist had taught her. She imagined herself walking—no, not walking, *striding*—confidently into the building and introducing herself to her new colleagues. It would be fine. She could do this. This was a safe environment. She had a plan and she had to believe things would go accordingly.

She gathered her bag, took a deep breath and opened her door very carefully, mindful of the pristine paintwork of the car beside her. She'd made it this far this morning, she'd found the strength to negotiate the LA traffic and now she was here. She held a conversation with herself in her head as she stepped out into the morning sun and followed the sign to the clinic. A short path took her to the front of the building and as she rounded the corner the vista took her breath away.

The view was incredible. The crisp, blue February

sky was clear of smog, just one of the bonuses of winter, and she could see over Los Angeles out to the coast where the Pacific Ocean shimmered in the morning sun. She turned her attention to the building itself. It was long and low, sleek and white. A massive wall of windows, shiny and gleaming, faced west, taking in the stunning view, and a semicircular driveway swept around in front of the glass separated from the building by a wide plaza bordered by sculpted, orderly, perfectly manicured gardens and hedges.

There was a low, unobtrusive sign of silver lettering on a white background that read 'The Hollywood Hills Clinic' in front of the building. Despite its name, the overall impression that she got was that she was about to step into a five-star resort, not a medical clinic. The sign didn't need to be large. Everyone who arrived here knew exactly where they were. No one's arrival at the clinic would be unplanned or unscheduled.

Her job interview had been conducted by phone and although she'd been on the internet and done her homework on the clinic and its management, nothing had prepared her for the reality. The first impression, from the exterior of the building alone, was definitely one of privilege, wealth and exclusivity.

Abi could see her reflection in the glass façade as she approached the front entrance and she self-consciously straightened her navy jacket and made sure her shirt was tucked into her pencil skirt. Her civilian clothes felt unfamiliar. The fabric was slippery and light compared to the thicker, more robust fabric of her army uniform and tended not to stay in place quite so firmly. Her low heels clicked on the pavers as she crossed the plaza area and she wondered if she was underdressed. If the luxury cars parked in the staff car park were any indication, she suspected her colleagues were going to be a hell of a lot more sophisticated than her. She suddenly felt like a country bumpkin on her first day in the big city.

You grew up in LA, she reminded herself. *You can do this. You are an excellent doctor, you will be a valuable member of staff.*

She didn't have to fit in; she just had to do a good job. She needed a job, this job, as her money wasn't going to last for ever and her psychologist had suggested, rather strongly, that it was time for her to start testing her reserves and her limits.

As the glass doors slid open Abi noticed a helicopter landing pad positioned at the far end of the building. It wasn't on the roof, neither was it tucked away discreetly out of sight, but instead it sat out the front, making a bold declaration that this was a place for the privileged and wealthy. Were people planning on making a statement as they arrived? That wouldn't surprise her given the sensational appearance of the clinic itself. The building alone certainly looked as though it was out to make a statement. Time would tell her what that statement was.

An expansive, modern foyer greeted her. A reception desk stood at one end in front of a wide window that looked out to the city below and on the opposite side of the foyer was a large courtyard with a central water feature and several oversized sculptures. More sculptures were displayed in the foyer itself and artworks hung from the walls. The look was reminiscent of a contemporary art gallery that had been merged with a very expensive and exclusive hotel. The artworks were beautifully lit and the foyer was sleek and modern.

She approached the reception desk, which was a long slab of marble. An enormous flower arrangement was positioned at one end and two chandeliers hung above it. The more Abi saw, the more the clinic looked like a five-star hotel—six-star, even, if there was such a thing. There wasn't much to indicate it was a medical facility. Even the woman behind the desk looked as if she had stepped out of a fashion magazine. Her hair was styled in a neat bob and her make-up had been expertly applied, and Abi felt more and more like the country cousin who expected to be evicted for not being glamorous enough.

She tried to ignore her misgivings as she introduced herself to the receptionist and explained that Freya Rothsberg was expecting her. Abi knew the clinic was owned by Freya and her brother, James. James was a world-renowned reconstructive surgeon who specialised in cosmetic surgery, and, from what Abi had discerned, Freya was responsible for the PR side of things. Freya had interviewed Abi over the phone but they were yet to meet.

'Welcome!' a woman called out loudly from several feet away. This must be Freya. She was about Abi's age, thirty or thereabouts, and of similar height, but that was about the extent of any resemblance. The closer Freya got the more the differences between them multiplied. Freya gave the immediate impression of someone who belonged here in the sun-kissed glamour of LA and the Hollywood Hills. She had a mane of dark hair that fell over her shoulders in natural surfer-chick waves. Her blue eyes were shining and her skin had a light tan, even at the end of winter. She had the typical LA cheerleader look—fit, trim and toned—and Abi doubted anything would have ever gone wrong in Freya Rothsberg's life.

In contrast to Freya's glowing Californian beauty Abi felt like a pale imitation of an LA woman, even though she had been born and bred here. Her dark brown hair with mahogany lights was cut just below her chin and had been softly feathered to frame her oval face. Her porcelain skin always looked like it had never seen the sun and Abi had never felt particularly pretty or noticeable. Her best, most striking feature were her eyes and she noted Freya's double-take when their eyes met as they introduced themselves. Abi was used to that reaction from people. Her eyes were a deep, rich amber, much like the glass eyes often found on a child's teddy bear. They were an unusual colour and she knew that was what people remembered about her.

'Hello, I'm Freya Rothsberg,' she said as she shook Abi's hand firmly. 'It's so nice to meet you! I hope you'll love it here at The Hills. Hold on one moment,' she said, 'there's someone I want to introduce you to.' A man entered the foyer and Freya called out to him. 'Damien!'

The man started walking towards them and Abi's first thought was that he was absolutely divine to look at. There was no other word to describe him. Was there no end to the beauty in this place?

He had designer stubble, brown eyes, so dark they were almost black, and a full head of black hair, short and spiky. He was tall, lean and looked like a model. His black suit might have been tailor-made for him rather than off the rack. No tie, open-collar shirt. Incredibly smooth, unlined skin.

'Abi,' Freya said as he reached them, 'this is Damien Moore, chief of reconstructive surgery.'

Abi recognised his name. This gorgeous man was her new boss. She found herself looking for telltale signs of plastic surgery and hoping not to find any, hoping it was just good genes because, despite working in the industry, she didn't find narcissistic men attractive. Not that she should care about what Damien Moore did with his body or his spare time.

'Damien, this is Abi Thompson, the new addition to your surgical team.'

'Dr Thompson.' He greeted her with a slight nod of his handsome head. Everything about him was dark and intense. Serious. He sounded totally controlled or was he just underwhelmed? Abi's lack of confidence made her question his expression before she could tell herself to relax. There was no reason for him to be unimpressed. He extended his hand but as Abi took it she felt a sharp shock as if there was a massive amount of static electricity between them. She felt as if her hand had been burnt and she withdrew it quickly, almost snatching it away, and resisted the temptation to check her palm for redness.

'You're a reconstructive and plastic surgeon?' he asked, apparently oblivious to the shock. Had he not felt it? 'Fully qualified?' he added, and Abi felt herself bristling.

What the hell did he mean by that?

'Of course,' she replied.

'Your résumé is very extensive.'

Was he accusing her of lying about her experience? Abi met his chilly stare head on and felt some of her old fire returning. 'If you'd like to fetch my application I'll wait and then we can compare notes.' She could feel the steam coming out of her ears and knew her amber eyes would be flashing angrily, but if she thought that would scare him into apologising she was mistaken. So she carried on. 'I have spent the past two years in Afghanistan, working in a CASH unit, putting soldiers back together. Making sure they have viable stumps for prosthetic limbs, repairing hands, sewing fingers back on that have been blown or shot off, holding chest walls together on the side of the road while under fire, so I think I'll be able to handle working here. I'm sure your facilities and your clients won't trouble me too much.' A combat support hospital may not be the equivalent of the five-star set-up currently surrounding her but Abi knew the surroundings were irrelevant. She was good at her job, very good, and she refused to let someone denigrate her skills.

Abi was aware that Freya was grinning and trying to suppress laughter but her cellphone rang before she could comment.

Freya glanced at the screen and apologised to them. 'It's Mila. I'm sorry but I have to take this. We have to finalise the plans for the function this weekend. Damien, would you mind giving Abi a quick tour of the clinic? I was going to do it but I'll catch up with you at morning tea instead.'

Abi hesitated as a slight sense of panic crept up on her. 'I don't mind waiting,' she said. It seemed a better option than going with Damien, who clearly wasn't impressed by her and who was putting her on edge. She didn't need to be stressed. Not on her first day. But Freya had already turned away to answer her phone, leaving Abi and Damien standing in silence, staring at each other.

'Looks like you're stuck with me.' The prospect

didn't seem to bother him. 'Come on, it'll give us a chance to get acquainted. To see if we'll be able to work well together.'

Not an overly pleasing prospect. Abi was feeling increasingly nervous about the decision she'd made to take the Hollywood Hills job. Perhaps it had been a mistake not to have had a face-to-face interview and checked out not only the facilities but her new colleagues too.

She needed to calm down, employ some of the coping strategies she'd been working on.

She took a deep breath and fought for composure. She needed to present a professional, controlled demeanour. It wouldn't do to fall to pieces in front of her new boss in the first five minutes of her first day.

'How much of the clinic did you see when you had your interview?' Damien asked her.

'This is the first time I've been here. My interview was conducted over the phone, that's why you read my résumé and why we haven't met.'

'I see. I've been on leave, I assumed this was all finalised while I was away. Didn't you want to see where you'd be working?'

'I know the clinic's reputation. That was enough for me.' In reality it was the closeted, safe and secure environment that she was most attracted to. She wasn't ready for a large public hospital. She didn't want to fight for funding or waste hours in meetings. She wasn't ready to deal with emergencies and chaos and shift work. She needed regular patterns and habits. She needed regular sleep too if she was to get her life back on track. Well-mannered, exclusive and polite was what she wanted and she hoped that this job would be a peaceful environment compared to public-hospital and defence-force work.

Damien showed her to her new office, which had light oak furniture, leather chairs and large picture windows with one-way blinds that looked out over Los Angeles. His office was beside hers and they shared a secretary who managed their appointment diary and theatre bookings. Damien introduced her to Jennifer and Abi expected that he would palm her off onto the secretary, but he surprised her by continuing her tour himself. Abi wasn't sure what to make of that. Was he being polite or was he going to use this as an opportunity to cross-examine her further about her experience?

Let him interrogate her, she decided. She'd answer any question he put to her.

He showed her through the rehabilitation area, which included a gym and hydrotherapy pools used by the physical therapists on staff, before taking her into the operating theatres. The facility was amazing. Absolutely no expense had been spared and Abi couldn't help but be impressed.

'Different from what you are used to?' Damien asked as he pushed open the swing door that led into an operating suite.

'We have state-of-the art equipment in the defence forces but those facilities don't extend past the medical necessities. The army certainly doesn't waste money on modern art and marble floors.'

'The Hills patients have high expectations,' he said with a light shrug of his designer-clad shoulders, 'not only of our expertise but of the service. They're LA's wealthy and they are used to having every whim catered for, and they have the same expectations when they walk through our doors as when they walk into a hotel or restaurant. They expect to be well looked after.'

Abi didn't care about the patients' expectations. The demands these patients would put on her would be nothing compared to what she'd put upon herself. In the army people got what they got, they had no expectations, the most important things were to keep them alive and maintain their function, but her expectations of her own skills was high. She knew she'd be able to handle the patients here. Operating on a millionaire would have to be less stressful than operating under fire. What she was interested in was a job that wasn't dangerous. She wanted peaceful. She *needed* peaceful. She knew she was going to get demanding but she was confident that she could cope. Stress presented in different ways and the pressure that she expected to encounter here, in civilised luxury, would be entirely different from the high stress in Afghanistan.

She was interested in a low-stress environment and one factor in keeping her stress levels down was knowing that the people she worked with were capable. It was time to ask Damien some questions of her own. 'How long have you worked here?'

'Two years.' He didn't volunteer anything further as he led the way out of the theatre suites. 'Our definitive observation unit is through there and the patient suites are around this way.'

They were six feet along the corridor when there was a crackle over the ceiling intercom.

'Code blue, room five. Repeat, code blue, room five.'

Damien took off. One minute he was next to her, the next he was gone, his long legs eating up the metres of the corridor and leaving Abi staring after him.

CHAPTER TWO

ABI LOOKED AT his retreating figure before she came to her senses and followed in his wake as the voice continued through the loudspeaker. 'Code blue, room five.'

Damien sprinted past the next two rooms before he shouldered open a door and Abi followed him into what was possibly the largest private hospital room she had ever seen. In the centre of the wall in front of them was an oversized hospital bed. A nurse was kneeling on the bed, delivering cardiac compressions to a young woman wearing pale pink silk pyjamas.

'She's in cardiac arrest. Unresponsive, not breathing, no pulse,' she told them as she continued with the compressions. She was doing a good job, delivering regular hard, deep compressions. The patient's shirt had been opened at the front and Abi was astounded at how underweight the woman was. She was so thin Abi could see each and every rib.

'Ellen, this is Dr Thompson,' Damien said, as he reached behind the bed and pushed on the wall. A small door that was set flush into the panelling popped open and he pulled a defibrillator from the alcove. And that was it by way of introductions. There was no time for anything more as he quickly tore open the packets and

Ellen sat back, stopping CPR, as Damien applied the adhesive electrodes to the patient's chest wall.

Abi watched as he connected the wires, flicked the machine on and pressed the 'analyse' button. The patient's heart rhythm appeared on the screen. She could see the disorganised pattern of ventricular fibrillation indicating that the brain was sending chaotic impulses to the heart that the heart couldn't interpret. This meant the heart couldn't fire a proper beat and it lost its rhythm and was unable to pump blood. The brain would be starved of oxygen, causing the patient to lose consciousness, and if the heart rhythm wasn't corrected the patient would die. Defibrillation to restore regular rhythm and normal contractions was the best way to stop ventricular fibrillation, and that was exactly what Damien was instigating.

The machine issued instructions in its automated voice.

Stop CPR, analysing.

Shock advised.

Abi could hear the whine as the power built up in the defibrillator unit.

Stand clear.

'Clear.' Damien repeated the machine's instructions to Abi and Ellen and checked to make sure they were well away from the patient before pressing the flashing red button. The machine delivered its first shock but there was no change in the rhythm of the heart.

Continue CPR.

'Ellen, can you get an IV line in, oxygen monitor and an Ambu bag,' Damien instructed, as he lowered the bed before continuing chest compressions.

Abi kicked off her shoes and stepped forward, ready

to help. She hitched her skirt up to give her room to move, wondering why on earth she'd thought it was a good idea to wear a suit, and climbed up on the bed. She tipped the patient's head back, opening her airway. She was ready to breathe for her the moment Damien paused in his compressions. They worked at a steady rate for two minutes until the AED machine interrupted them.

Stop CPR, analysing.

Shock advised.

'Clear.' Damien repeated the process to deliver a second shock.

Their patient was pale and clammy and she was start-ing to go a little blue around the mouth and jaw. Abi and Damien continued another round of CPR but this time Abi used the Ambu bag, squeezing air into the patient's lungs after each set of thirty compressions. Another two minutes passed.

Stop CPR, analysing.

Shock advised.

They stood clear again as once more Damien pressed the red flashing button and this time a normal heart rhythm was restored.

Abi's shoulders sagged as she slid off the bed and all three of them breathed a collective sigh of relief as they watched the heartbeat on the little screen.

Ellen removed the electrodes of the AED and re-placed them with ECG leads as a second team, who Abi could only assume were the resus team, moved further into the room. Abi hadn't noticed their arrival in all the chaos and they departed as swiftly and si-lently as they had arrived. Accompanied by Ellen, they wheeled the patient out of the room, no doubt taking her to the definitive observation unit, and Abi was left alone with Damien.

Now that the drama was over she didn't know where to look or what to do. She stood in the middle of the room and tried to avoid looking at Damien. She studied her surroundings instead. The oversized hospital bed was gone but the room was far from empty. In front of a large window that overlooked a courtyard was a carpeted lounge area complete with a leather sofa, an armchair upholstered in a rich cream fabric and a marble-topped coffee table. She wandered over to the window, the carpet thick and plush under her stockinged feet, and took in the view over the courtyard. It offered complete privacy but even so the glass was tinted. Abi could see out but no one could see in. An en-suite bathroom was tucked into the far corner of the room and Abi could just glimpse a marble vanity in the mirrored reflection. The medical equipment was all tucked away discreetly, Abi assumed into purpose-built storage, and the room looked and felt like a hotel suite. The surroundings might be very different to what she was used to but the patients were the same. They all had lives that needed to be improved, or even saved, and that was her job. It didn't matter if they were civilian or military, she just had to do what she was trained for.

'Thanks for your help.' Damien was standing beside her. 'It was a good outcome,' he added with a slight nod of his head.

Was that all the acknowledgement she was going to get?

She supposed she was only doing her job, she didn't need to be congratulated for that, but she felt a little short-changed that he wasn't more effusive, particularly after his previous criticism and questions relating to her medical qualifications. Surely she'd put some of his doubts to rest now?

She was pleased with how she'd coped. She hadn't panicked, hadn't felt stressed, she'd simply just clicked into gear. Her medical skills were as precise as ever. It was like riding a bike and she was thrilled to know that she hadn't lost her touch in that regard. Her personal life might be a disaster, her self-belief might have taken a pounding and she might be struggling to cope out in the big wide world, but in the familiar environment of a hospital it seemed she'd lost none of her confidence. It was a reassuring discovery but it didn't take away the disappointment that Damien didn't seem quite so impressed.

'I'd like to retract my earlier comment,' he added.

'What?'

'When I questioned your qualifications. I jumped to conclusions and I'm sorry for that.'

'Thank you.' That was all she'd wanted. Some recognition of a job well done. Her day had just got a little bit brighter.

She could do this.

'It's obvious you can think on your feet and cope under pressure. Your defence-force experience means that you are undoubtedly qualified to cope with anything we can throw at you, as you've capably demonstrated, and I apologise,' he said, and then he smiled.

Abi's knees went weak. She sat down hard on the sofa as she tried to pretend that it was the adrenalin from the resuscitation that was flooding her system and making her knees wobble but she knew it was Damien's smile. Suddenly he lost his serious, intense expression.

His smile transformed his face and now he looked like a man who knew how to have a good time, who knew how to laugh.

'Come on,' he said, 'let's grab a coffee and catch our breath. We can finish the tour later.'

He extended his hand to help her up from the sofa and the touch of his palm as Abi placed her hand in his created a current of electricity so strong that it couldn't be contained and it shot out of her to ignite the air surrounding them until it seemed to glow. She could feel the air around them moving. It crackled and swirled like a living, breathing entity, creating a fire that sucked the air from her lungs and made it impossible to breathe. She pulled herself up on wobbly legs. Her vision was blurred around the edges and she felt dizzy and light headed. She couldn't seem to catch her breath.

'Are you okay?' Damien asked as he let go of her hand.

Released from his hold, abruptly disconnected from him, she found she was able to breathe again. 'I'm fine,' she said, as she smoothed down the front of her skirt and stepped into her shoes. She closed her eyes briefly and took a quick deep breath to make sure she really was all right before she followed him out of the room. As they walked along the corridor she made sure she kept a couple of feet between them. Touching him again was out of the question.

Damien drank his coffee as quickly as possible without being impolite. He had taken Abi into the staff kitchen to make coffee but the room felt too small for both of them. He was having trouble breathing and it had nothing to do with the emergency he'd just averted and everything to do with a slim brunette who sat opposite him. He'd been dismissive of her without cause earlier and he felt badly about that, but now he was having trouble remembering exactly what his issue had been.

He could smell fresh peaches and he knew that was her fragrance he was inhaling. Was it any wonder he was having difficulty breathing? Every breath was like inhaling the essence of Abi and it was sweet torture. She made him think of the golden days of summer. Her amber eyes glowed like the late afternoon sun and she shimmered as if there was an energy within her that was too big to contain, although a sixth sense told him that something had happened that had diminished her glow. Something had damaged her, something had given her an air of fragility. She was only a waif of a girl but it wasn't just about her size and he wondered what had happened in her past. But he didn't have the time or energy to worry about her psyche; he had enough of his own issues to deal with. He didn't have time for distractions and that was what she was.

He needed to breathe, he needed to leave.

He drained the dregs of his coffee, pushed his chair back and stood. 'Will you be able to find your way back to your office? I need to speak to Freya.' He knew he was making excuses but he needed to get away. He needed to break the spell he could feel her casting over him.

His departure was abrupt, and he could see from Abi's puzzled expression that she thought so too but she didn't complain or argue. She just nodded silently. It appeared she wasn't much of a talker.

He did genuinely want to speak to Freya—he felt she needed to know about Clementine Jones, though he knew she would have heard the alarm and the code-blue call—but he suffered a moment of guilt over his hasty exit. He pushed those thoughts to one side as he knocked on Freya's door and then brought her up to speed on the emergency.

'Clementine was booked in for a breast enlargement but she has a long-standing eating disorder that probably triggered her cardiac arrest. She's in the DOU under Geoff's care now, but she needs counselling. I know you're only taking on a handful of clients but this girl needs to be included on your list. She's playing Russian roulette at the moment. It's only a matter of time before she's a statistic instead of a person. If she won't see you then she needs to see another psychologist. James is her admitting surgeon but I'm sure he'll agree.'

Freya nodded. 'I'll take care of it.' She tilted her head to one side. 'So you were first on the scene?'

'With Abi.' He had to give credit where it was due.

'You resuscitated her together?'

Damien nodded.

'Now do you think she can handle the job?'

He needed Abi to pull her weight. He'd fought to have an extra surgeon on staff to ease some of his caseload but his first impressions had worried him. He hadn't thought her old enough or strong enough to help him but he had to admit he had revised his opinion. He would give her the benefit of the doubt now after the composure she had displayed during the emergency. 'I'll agree I'm more confident now,' he replied.

'Good.' Freya nodded. 'Because James wants her to assist you in Theatre tomorrow. That will give her a feel for how the clinic runs and also give you a chance to assess her skills. Once you're happy we'll start to give her patients of her own, which will free up some of your time.'

Damien was happy with that. He was exhausted and had far too much on his plate. There were far too many things fighting for his attention. He had too much else to think about at the moment. He was virtually a single parent, raising a young daughter, and he had more work than he could handle. He couldn't work twenty-four-seven—it wasn't feasible and it was not what he wanted. Abi's appointment needed to be successful. She had to work out and if she didn't she'd have to go. It was as simple as that.

Abi's head was spinning as she pulled her 4x4 into the driveway and hit the button for the automatic garage door. She needed time to think about her day and what had happened. What she'd seen, what she'd done, who she'd met. She would collect Jonty and they'd go for a walk. That would give her time to sort through her thoughts on the clinic, on Freya and on Damien.

The motor of the garage door made a distinctive whine as it kicked into gear and Abi could see Jonty racing across the lawn to greet her as she eased her car forward. A wave of guilt washed over her as she saw how eager he was to welcome her home. This was the first day that she and Jonty had been parted. She wondered if his day had been less eventful than hers. Was this how working mothers felt? At least she'd organised company for him. He shouldn't have been lonely but she still hoped he'd missed her.

She closed the door and made a beeline for her landlords' bungalow at the front of the property. Her landlords, George and Irma, were a retired couple in their late sixties and Abi rented their converted garage apartment. She had moved in about six weeks ago and had since found herself adopted by George and Irma as part of the family. She didn't mind; she was enjoying feeling like she was part of a family. They had adopted her dog too, offering to keep him company while Abi returned to work. She wished she'd been able to take Jonty with her, for her sake more than his, but the clinic was no place for a large, hairy, golden retriever.

'How did your first day go?' Irma asked as Abi stepped onto the back porch. 'Not quite what I expected,' she replied. 'But I'm sure it will be okay.' She still needed time to process the day's events. The Hills was different from what she was used to, very different, and even if she wasn't sure that she would be suited to working there she suspected it would be interesting, albeit slightly more routine than the army. But perhaps that was just what she needed—ordinary and routine, excluding the odd cardiac arrest, of course.

'I've made an extra-large pot of chilli beef. Would you like to eat with us tonight? You must be tired.'

Abi was more than happy to be looked after by Irma. She knew her fridge was bare and dinner at her place was likely to be toast and maybe a packet soup. But more than the dinners it was the feeling that someone was interested in her and cared enough to make sure she was fed. She'd never experienced that on a regular basis. Growing up, her family life had been erratic, to say the least. Swings and roundabouts. Her mother had done her best at times but she really hadn't coped with the real world and Abi didn't remember her father. And army life, while she'd been looked after, she suspected was also very different to normal family life. George and Irma missed the company of their children and Abi enjoyed filling that void. It was nice to feel normal.

'That sounds delicious. Have I got time to take Jonty for a quick walk first?'

'Of course.'

Above the garage George had added a bedroom, small bathroom and a kitchen/living area that opened out onto a deck that overlooked a small park. Jonty loved exploring the park but Abi avoided it once the sun had set. She needed milk for her morning coffee so she changed quickly into a pair of black exercise leggings, a long-sleeved black T-shirt and a bright pink, puffy, padded, insulated vest. She wrapped an orange scarf around her neck, shoved her phone and some coins into her pocket and clipped Jonty's lead to his collar. They'd make a quick dash to the mini-mart two blocks away. She let Jonty go to the toilet before they left as once he had his coat on he would know not to stop unless she directed him to. She fastened his coat around his body and headed out to the street.

Jonty had been assigned to Abi on her return from Afghanistan, on her psychologist's recommendation. According to Caroline, many of her patients who had been diagnosed with post-traumatic stress disorder found that an assistance dog brought enormous benefits, and Abi had to admit that she was grateful for Jonty's companionship. She'd never had a dog, she'd never had any pets before, but she had very quickly grown attached to Jonty. She was a dog person, she'd decided.

Jonty had been assigned to help calm her and to increase her confidence in her ability to cope with the outside world, but nervousness still made her heart rate increase as they approached the supermarket. Ever since the incident in Afghanistan she had been exceedingly nervous in new or crowded environments until she'd had a chance to check out the lie of the land.

She quickly scanned the interior of the shop and only when she could see that it was relatively quiet, with few customers, did she step inside, taking Jonty with her. He was allowed to accompany her so long as he was wearing the coat that identified him as an assistance dog. They headed to the milk fridge at the back of the store, Abi wishing, not for the first time, that the shop-keeper would keep the milk near the front. Having to go to the far corner of the store always bothered her, even though she knew where the emergency exit was.

A dark-haired man stood in front of the open fridge door. He was reaching for the same milk that Abi wanted. She thought about asking him to grab one for her too but that would mean initiating a conversation with a stranger. Even with Jonty beside her she wasn't comfortable doing that. She waited as the man closed the fridge door and turned around.

'Dr Thompson!'

Abi's heart skipped a beat as a voice that had become almost familiar in just one day uttered her name. She lifted her eyes.

He was tall and lean. His thick black hair was expertly styled to look effortlessly casual and a day's worth of stubble darkened his square jaw and contrasted with the smooth olive skin of his forehead and cheeks. He was watching her with eyes so dark they were almost black. He was gorgeous.

Damien.

His serious expression vanished, to be replaced by

his wide smile, showcasing perfect white teeth. Did this man have any physical flaws?

'You need milk?' he asked.

'For my coffee,' she replied, as if he'd care why she needed it.

He took a second carton from the fridge and passed it to her, not checking which one she wanted. 'Do you live near here?'

'A couple of blocks that way,' she said, pointing east.

'We're two blocks south.'

She wondered who 'we' meant. Was he married? He didn't wear a wedding ring.

She glanced at his left hand, double-checking, but she knew she was right. What she didn't know was when she'd noticed and why. Not that it mattered. Lots of surgeons didn't wear rings and his marital status was of no concern to her.

'Is this your dog?'

She nodded. 'This is Jonty.'

'An assistance dog?'

'It's a project I'm involved with,' she said. She didn't see any need to mention that the project was personal and involved trying to fix her fragile psyche. There was no need to mention that her psychologist had recommended the programme. She didn't intend to share tales about her private life with her new boss.

Finding out he was practically her neighbour was enough to deal with. He didn't need to know anything more about her. She was used to mixing her work and her social life, there wasn't another option in the military really, but things had changed recently. She had changed. She had become more reserved, more introverted, and that was part of the reason that Caroline had suggested Jonty. She'd hoped it would help to restore Abi's confidence and alleviate some of her fears about the world. Bad things weren't always going to happen. Abi needed to experience the world and remember the good things.

Damien insisted on paying for her milk, along with his own, and they left the shop together. As they stepped onto the pavement he pulled a set of keys from his pocket and pressed a button. Abi heard the sound of doors unlocking and saw the lights flash on a black, luxury SUV that was parked out the front of the shop. 'Can I give you a lift?' he offered.

It seemed he had the charming personality to match his very appealing features. But Abi knew how dangerous a weapon charm could be in a good-looking man. She looked at his car. There was not a speck of dirt or a scratch or dent on it. Its paintwork was immaculate and it suited him. It was shiny, sleek perfection and so different from her old soft-top. She couldn't imagine hopping into something so tidy, let alone putting her hairy, thirty-kilogram companion in there too. Had he forgotten about Jonty?

'No, thank you. We need the exercise.' And she needed more time to think.

He was good-looking and charming, there was no denying that, but that was no reason to let him drive her home. She'd had good-looking, charming bosses before and things hadn't turned out so well for her the last time. In fact, things had gone terribly pear-shaped and she was still recovering. She needed time to herself, time to heal. There was no room in her life or in her head for anything other than surviving. Her goal was to achieve emotional stability and financial security. She didn't need any complications and she knew all too well how complicated men could make things. Besides, he was part of a 'we' and that was all she needed to know about him to ensure she kept her distance. Single men were one thing but men with other commitments were definitely off her list. That was one path she knew she would avoid at all costs. Being pleasant at work was one thing, mixing socially was another, but men with baggage were a definite no.

CHAPTER THREE

ABI ARRIVED AT The Hills on her second day wearing her smartest dress, a simple black jersey wrap, and nude-colored heels. She had a thin gold chain around her neck but she still wasn't sure if she was dressed smartly enough. Freya had arranged a morning tea yesterday to introduce Abi to everyone and all the staff she had met had seemed extraordinarily beautiful and impressively well-dressed.

She supposed it made sense given that the clinic serviced the wealthy and elite of Los Angeles society but she wasn't sure how, or if, she measured up by comparison. She suspected both her wardrobe and her looks were severely lacking and decided she'd have to wow them with her medical talents instead.

She found her way to her office, where she was greeted by Jennifer, the secretary who took care of her and Damien, and the news that Damien had requested an eight-thirty meeting.

A white doctor's coat was hanging behind her office door. Still unsure about her outfit, she took the coat off the hook and slipped it over her clothes. She would feel more comfortable and in control if she was already in scrubs but this would have to do. Perhaps she could engineer her diary to ensure she spent most of her time in Theatre—she felt at home in that environment and in that uniform. She checked her reflection in the mirror on the wall and saw that the coat had The Hills' intertwined double H logo monogrammed on the breast pocket. Like everything else in the clinic, even the coats had been taken to the next level.

Damien's door was open. She took a moment to check him out before she knocked. He was wearing a different suit today, dark navy with a pale blue shirt and a red silk tie embroidered with blue fleurs-de-lis, but he still looked as if he'd stepped out of the pages of a fashion magazine. Abi pulled the white coat more firmly around her as she knocked and entered. Her whole outfit had cost no more than a hundred dollars; Damien's tie alone had probably cost twice that.

There was a coffee waiting for her and Damien slid it across his desk as she sank into the leather seat by the window. His office was identical to hers in size and also looked out onto an internal courtyard complete with a bubbling water feature that had a stunning metal sculpture as its centrepiece. Everything about this place was slick and professional and for the first time since the previous day Abi relaxed slightly. It would be nice to be associated with this clinic. This move could turn out to be a good decision and having something work out right for her would be a pleasant change.

'Milk?' he asked, making a reference to their unexpected meeting last night. His voice was deep but it lightened when he smiled. She'd noticed how it changed with his mood, from serious surgeon to friendly colleague to charming shopper, and she wondered which one was the real Damien.

She nodded but Damien was already adding it for her. 'Do you know how our patient from yesterday is? Clementine?' she queried. She'd been worried all night about the young woman who'd gone into cardiac arrest.

'She's in a stable condition. I just spoke to Geoff, our cardiologist. He's monitoring her closely but he's happy. She wasn't physically strong enough to undergo surgery so, in a way, this is not a bad outcome. She's had a long-standing eating disorder that her parents thought was being managed but it appears not. Clementine needs to agree to get more help,' Damien replied.

'What was she booked in for?'

'A breast enlargement,' Damien explained. 'James had been delaying her operation, telling her she had to put on weight because her body wouldn't cope with an anaesthetic, but I have no idea if this episode will make any difference. From what I understand, she's had intervention and therapy many times before. Freya is going to see her with her psychologist's hat on— she has a special interest in patients who have eating disorders—but if Clementine isn't receptive she'll be transferred to another facility. Apparently Clementine wants to stay here and her parents have agreed so that will be the carrot Freya dangles.'

James Rothsberg was the head of the clinic and also a reconstructive and plastic surgeon, and Abi was re-lieved to hear that he had put the patient's well-being first but surprised to hear that Clementine had been scheduled for a breast enlargement. 'Do you do a lot of cosmetic surgery here?'

'We are in Hollywood.'

'I realise that.'

'It's not all we do,' Damien continued, 'but you're

assisting me in Theatre today and it's what's on our list and what I wanted to talk to you about.'

'We're doing cosmetic surgery? That's not what I expected.' She was a specialist in the field of plastic and reconstructive surgery but her experience was in the reconstructive side of things. Cosmetic surgery wasn't her forte.

'It's awards season in Hollywood,' Damien said as he shrugged his shoulders in his bespoke suit jacket. 'The film industry awards are only twelve days away, which makes this our busiest time of the year. Everyone wants something done without anyone knowing about it. James can't possibly keep up with the demand so I lend a hand.

'Don't worry, no one will know you've relaxed your ethics,' he added, making her wonder if he'd had another look at her résumé and refreshed his knowledge of her background. 'The celebrities don't want anyone to know they've had surgical assistance to look their best on awards night. We have a lot of rather wealthy and sometimes reclusive patients who demand privacy and anonymity. They won't mention your name and they expect the same consideration from you.'

He smiled again and Abi's breath caught in her throat. 'All your recognition will come from your reconstructive work and there will be plenty of that. We have an arrangement with the Bright Hope Clinic to do some charitable work for the underprivileged children who are treated there and that, along with the other external referrals that come to us for reconstructive surgery, will keep you occupied most of the time. But this cosmetic work on the celebrities and their partners, and the Hollywood heavy hitters and their mistresses, wives and girlfriends, and the cash they are prepared to part with for the best medical care and for our discretion means that we are able to do that charity work, and I suspect that will appeal to you.

'You will get paid for any charity work that you do but The Hills, by which I mean James, absorbs those expenses. We are strong believers in giving back to the community. It's a win-win situation. So, does that make you feel better about today's list?'

Abi nodded. She hadn't really thought about the ramifications of the clinic's location on the client base but Damien's explanation did ease her conscience. Besides, the surgical procedures were the same no matter what you called them. Although the surgeries were performed for different reasons, aesthetics or function, the actual operations were similar and giving them labels such as cosmetic or reconstructive was really just semantics.

'Okay,' Damien continued, 'on today's list we have two blepharoplasties, one neck lift, two liposuctions, a breast lift and an arm lift. I have to warn you, a couple of our patients are men. One is a very well-known actor who has decided to treat himself to a neck lift and the other patient has recently left his wife and is planning on unveiling his much younger girlfriend at the awards and he wants to take a few years off his face with an eyelid lift. But remember, discretion is something we guarantee at The Hills and I know it's been written into your contract but I need to know that you can rock a poker face. It doesn't matter what we think about cosmetic surgery, these patients have their reasons for undergoing this work and we need to be discreet and respectful.'

Abi had plenty of her own insecurities. While she

didn't think she'd ever resort to cosmetic surgery, as her insecurities weren't really physical, she could understand people's need to change or to make a better version of themselves to boost their confidence, and she wasn't going to judge them for their choices. She understood that different things worked for different people and she certainly wouldn't criticise a patient's decision, although, given the opportunity, she thought she might try to dissuade some of the people some of the time.

She wondered what the clinic's policy on that was. Was honesty considered the best policy or was the bottom line the main consideration? But she wasn't going to ask that question on her second day. She would toe the line for the moment, there would be time to find out later just how much she was expected to keep her opinion to herself.

'Don't worry about me,' she said as she finished her coffee. 'I understand how this works.'

The day ran smoothly and the time passed quickly, as it always seemed to when she was immersed in surgery. She was impressed with Damien's skill but also with the way he related to the theatre staff. He treated everyone with respect and she could tell that the nurses adored him. She had done a large percentage of each of the surgeries under Damien's watchful eye and he'd been encouraging and complimentary about her skills. As far as she could tell, there was not a vast difference between cosmetic surgery and regular reconstructive surgery, although it was perhaps *always* important to make sure the stitches were as tiny and neat as possible, and preferably hidden, in all cosmetic procedures. But neat stitching was one thing she had always prided herself on.

They were finishing off the second blepharoplasty and there was one more surgery still to come when the theatre phone rang. The blepharoplasty was something different for Abi. She was used to repairing eyelids, stitching eye injuries and even, on one occasion, making a new eyelid, but to do an eyelid lift purely to make someone look younger was novel.

The scrub nurse had answered the phone and Abi could see her looking at Damien. 'Dr Moore, it's for you, it's your daughter's school. Apparently no one has come to collect her.'

He had a daughter?

She didn't know why she was so surprised. She knew he was a 'we' but a daughter was more than she'd expected.

'Can you finish up for me, Dr Thompson?' Damien asked as he tied off the last stitch. Abi glanced at the clock on the theatre wall. It was already after four in the afternoon and she wondered what he was planning on doing. 'She needs ointment applied to her eyelids before they are bandaged,' he continued.

'I can do it,' the theatre nurse offered. Abi wasn't sure if she was offering because she saw Abi's vague expression and took pity on her or whether she was trying to get into Damien's good graces, but Abi wasn't about to let her take over. She could do this.

'I've got it,' she said.

She listened in to Damien's conversation as she applied the ointment. He could have taken the call on another phone but he seemed quite happy to have the conversation in front of the staff.

'This is Dr Moore,' Damien said, as the scrub nurse held the phone to his ear. He could feel the pressure building in his chest as anger rose in him. What was Brooke up to now? She was supposed to be collecting Summer from school. Had she forgotten again? What was the point of making arrangements with her if she was so unreliable? He worked hard to accommodate his ex-wife, he wanted to make sure that their daughter got to spend time with both of them, but sometimes Brooke made it impossible.

'Summer hasn't been collected,' the woman on the end of the phone told him. 'She has been sent to after-school care and I need to notify you. I need to make sure she is picked up by six o'clock.'

'I've been in surgery all day, I'm *still* in surgery and I won't be finished by then.' Damien was aware that all the theatre staff could hear his conversation quite clearly but it was too late for secrets now. Abi was busy bandaging their patient's eyes but he could sense by her posture that she was listening just as intently as all the others, but he couldn't worry about them. Summer was his priority, now and always. 'Have you contacted her mother? She was supposed to collect her.'

'Of course, but she is in New York.'

'What? She's *where*?' God, that woman was unbelievable. What the hell was she doing in New York?

'She told me she contacted you.'

'What? No, she hasn't,' he said, but he knew what she would have done. She would have left a message on his cellphone. No matter how many times he told her he didn't check his cell if he was in Theatre, she never listened. Brooke always danced to her own tune; other people's lives were of no consequence to her, she didn't make allowances or exceptions for any of them, not even her own daughter. Once again, Damien would have to pick up the pieces left by Brooke's selfishness. 'Can you give me five minutes?' he asked the woman on the phone. 'I'll make some arrangements and call you back.'

He nodded to the scrub nurse to hang up the phone and let out another expletive.

'What's going on?' the theatre nurse asked.

'Summer hasn't been collected from school,' he replied. He had another couple of hours left in Theatre and just five minutes to work out a solution. He wouldn't be finished before six so he wouldn't be finished in time to collect Summer.

His eyes roamed the room as he tried to figure out what to do. Abi taped the last bandage in place and looked up just as his gaze settled on her. She might just be the answer to his problem.

'Abi, do you think you could do me a favour?' he asked.

Damien looked worried, stressed, and Abi thought it was probably best that he didn't operate while in this state. 'Sure,' she replied without hesitation, expecting he was going to ask her to start his final surgery, but his question when he asked it was completely unexpected.

'Would you collect Summer for me?'

'What?' Was he crazy? Surely he was kidding. 'I've never met your daughter,' she retorted, but even in her flustered state she realised there was something he hadn't considered. 'I doubt the school would send her home with a complete stranger. Why don't you go and I'll start the last case?'

'The last case is a breast lift.'

Abi knew that, she was supposed to assist for that surgery too.

'How many of those have you done?' he asked, and judging by his tone she knew he already knew the answer.

Exactly none. She stared at Damien and her silence was all the answer he needed.

'That's what I thought. I need to finish off here. Would you please collect her?'

'Why doesn't Summer's mother pick her up?'

'That's a good question,' he replied with a sigh. 'She was supposed to but apparently she is on her way to New York.'

Apparently? 'New York? Didn't you know?' Had it just slipped his mind that his wife was away and he was supposed to be picking up his daughter? Was it something he forgot on a regular basis and now he was trying to make it her problem?

Abi didn't think so. It didn't seem to fit with his character and he seemed to be genuinely upset and to be struggling for solutions. She believed this had come out of the blue for him too.

Damien shook his head. 'Brooke told the school that she told me I would have to make arrangements but I haven't heard from her. This is the third time she has done this.'

'What did you do the other times?' she asked, as the anaesthetist began to reverse the anaesthetic.

'Once I collected her and another time she went home with a friend. But school finished forty-five minutes ago so those mothers would have left, and I don't have any of their numbers. Please, Abi, I wouldn't ask you if I had any other options. My daughter is five years old. You remember being five, don't you? I don't want her to feel abandoned.'

That word cut Abi to the core. *Abandoned* was the one word to use if he wanted her sympathy and co-operation. But he couldn't have known that. That would be impossible. It had just been a comment. But of course she remembered being five.

She also remembered having no one to pick her up. Day after day she would get herself home from school. On a good day it had been because her mother had been working, but on a bad day her mother would be passed out on the sofa, hungover or drunk.

Abi had had no one to rely on when she'd been five or seven or nine. She'd had no one until she'd joined the army at seventeen and had gone to medical school. She'd had no one really until she'd met Mark and even then she'd still ended up alone. There had never been anyone she could rely on. She knew exactly what Damien was talking about.

She started to cave in. 'I'd do it but I really don't think the school would let me.'

Damien had an answer for that. 'I'll ring them and I'll get Freya to email your staff ID photo to the office. You'll just have to show some ID when you get there. Please? I don't know what else to do. The school is ten minutes from home. If you could just pick her up and I'll collect her from your place as soon as I'm done here.'

He knew she lived in his neighbourhood, which would put her home close to the school. His plan made sense but Abi didn't know if she could do it, although it was hard to refuse when he was looking so distressed and imploring her with his dark, dark eyes. If she acquiesced she knew it would be stressful. Could she handle it?

But she remembered what it felt like to be five years

old and know that no one was coming for you, knowing that you were on your own. She'd hated that feeling and she knew she couldn't put someone else in that position.

She sighed and said, 'Let me make a call.' She threw her gloves and mask into the bin as Damien signed the surgical notes. She was careful not to agree to his crazy plan just yet. She still didn't know if she was capable of agreeing to his suggestion. She needed a second opinion. She needed to run it past her psychologist but that wasn't a conversation she was prepared to have in public. She pushed open the door into the scrub room and went to fetch her cellphone.

She dialled the emergency number, the one Caroline had promised to always answer. Abi wasn't sure what Caroline termed an *emergency* exactly but, for her, going unprepared into a new environment that was not only large but filled with people and knowing she would have to introduce herself to strangers without time for any research or reconnaissance definitely fell into the *emergency assistance* category. Abi had no idea how she was going to manage this and she needed Caroline to give her some contingencies to help her cope.

Caroline answered on the third ring and Abi explained the situation.

'I assume,' Caroline said, after listening to Abi's predicament, 'that you would actually like to do this favour for your boss?'

Would she? Part of her worried that if she agreed she would be setting a precedent and part of her also worried that she was letting him take advantage of her. But she could also remember what it was like to be left to find her own way home because her mother was incapable, again. Back then nobody had noticed if you weren't collected from school, lots of kids made their own way home, but not many primary school children had that freedom now. They were bundled off to after-school care before anything untoward could happen to them. Abi remembered all too well that feeling of abandonment and if she could help by collecting Summer she would. It didn't matter that Summer didn't know her; she imagined just knowing her dad had sent someone would be better than being forgotten. Abi wasn't doing this for Damien.

'I'm not doing this for my boss, I'm doing it for his daughter,' she explained. 'She was expecting her mother to collect her and I don't want her to feel that she's not important.' Abi knew that Caroline understood her reasons and where they stemmed from. They'd been over a lot of old, and new, ground together and Abi didn't have many secrets left that Caroline hadn't heard. Damien, however, was a new topic and not one they'd discussed, and neither did she intend to. Abi felt it was best, safest to leave him in the category of work colleague. There was no reason to go into any detail about him, he was of no consequence. 'But I have never met Summer, I don't know the school, I don't know the staff and they don't know me. It's making me nervous.'

'The school is close to your house, though?' Caroline asked.

'Yes.'

'Why don't you go home and collect Jonty?' the psychologist suggested. 'Take him with you. You'll feel better and if Summer likes dogs it will break the ice with her too.'

Abi took a deep breath. She could do this. 'That's a good idea. Thanks.'

She felt better when she ended the call, far more confident. This might just work.

Abi pulled her 4x4 into the school car park. The building was long and low and stretched out before her, but fortunately the car park was virtually empty and she was able to put her car two places from the front entrance. She took a moment to survey her surroundings, not that she really expected any danger but it was a habit she had formed over the past six months and it was proving hard to shake. There was no one around and she could see nothing suspicious. She was in the middle of suburban LA, she reminded herself. It wasn't Kabul and she was unlikely to encounter a suicide bomber here. But her paranoia still got the better of her and she reached across to her right and opened the passenger door, letting Jonty jump out first. He sniffed the air and once she was certain he was showing no signs of distress she took a deep breath and stepped out of the car.

She showed her ID at the office and was taken to the after-school-hours area, where about two dozen kids were engaged in various activities. She spotted Summer straight away. Three girls were jumping rope and one of the girls turning the rope was a miniature, female version of Damien. Dressed in pink she had her dark hair tied in two short pigtails that stuck out from the sides of her head but there was no mistaking that gene pool.

'Summer,' the school secretary called to her, getting her attention. 'This is Dr Thompson. She works with your father and she's come to collect you.'

'Please, call me Abi. And this is Jonty.'

'A dog! You brought a dog in.' All three girls, Summer and her two friends, immediately surrounded Abi.

Jonty lapped up the attention. Caroline's advice to bring him had been spot on.

Abi took a closer look at Summer as the girls patted Jonty. She had the same oval face, the same dark eyes and the same smile as her father. She was as cute as a button.

She seemed to have no qualms going home with Abi. She skipped along beside Jonty and was far from the forlorn, lonely figure Abi had been expecting. If she knew her father had forgotten to collect her, it didn't seem to bother her. What Abi saw was a confident, happy five-year-old who was very comfortable with strangers. Summer was not at all what she had envisaged.

Abi opened the car door and tilted the passenger seat forward. Jonty jumped in and Abi reset the seat and waited for Summer to climb up into the passenger seat, but she was standing still, her head tilted to one side, as she seemed to be considering something.

'Are you going to get in?' Abi asked her.

'Are you sure you're a doctor?' Summer replied.

'I'm positive. Why?'

'You have a very old car.'

If Summer had visited The Hills and seen the cars driven by the doctors who worked there, Abi could understand the question. She didn't have that kind of money. Not yet. While money did motivate her, she had grown up poor and didn't plan on staying poor; she couldn't, however, imagine spending a small fortune on a car. She had other priorities. She wanted to have the security of her own house and some investments, and a brand-new car was not on that list, but she wasn't about to explain all that to a five-year-old.

'It's just me and Jonty,' she said. 'He's very hairy and sometimes very dirty. I don't have to worry about him messing up this car.'

'Oh, okay. Does the top come off?' she asked, as she climbed in and continued to chatter away, keeping up an almost one-sided conversation for the short drive to Abi's house. Summer certainly wasn't shy, but despite the fact that there didn't appear to be any need for Abi to have left work to rush over here to rescue a child who didn't need her she didn't mind. Summer was delightful and it was nice to have some two-legged company.

But, of course, Abi hadn't factored in the after-school snack. She had no food in her apartment other than an apple that was more than likely past its use-by date and a box of breakfast cereal. She couldn't recall the last time she'd done a proper grocery shop. She was not all that conscious about food as she didn't have a big appetite. Growing up, there had never been enough to eat in her house and therefore food had never been a focus. Before she'd joined the army she couldn't ever recall eating three meals a day.

She decided the best course of action would be to take Summer over to her landlords. Irma always had something sweet to eat, usually fresh from her oven, and today was no exception. Abi let Irma fuss over them and feed them both, and once Summer's hunger pains had been satisfied the little girl asked, with her mouth full of one of Irma's cookies, 'Can we take Jonty for a walk?'

'Just a short one,' Abi told her, 'before it gets dark.'

Irma pressed a couple of extra cookies into Summer's hand to take with her as Abi clipped Jonty's lead on.

'I'd like a dog,' Summer announced, as they hit the footpath. 'Or a little brother.'

'A dog might be better,' Abi replied. 'Little brothers can be annoying.'

'Do you have a brother?' Summer asked.

Abi shook her head. 'No, nor a sister.'

'How do you know they're annoying, then?'

Abi laughed. Summer made a fair point. 'Good question. I'm just guessing, I suppose.'

'It'll have to be a dog. Mum doesn't want any more children. She says she didn't even want me.'

Abi had no idea what the right response to this statement was. Her experience with children was limited at best. Should she make a big deal of Summer's comment? Tell her she must be mistaken? But she couldn't do that, she didn't know the facts. For all she knew, Summer could be speaking the truth. Why would she make something like that up? What child would think like that unless they'd heard those words uttered? Abi felt as though her heart was breaking. No one deserved to hear that from their mother. Abi's mother had loved her, she just hadn't been able to care for her properly. Her addictions and her circumstances had made that impossible, but what was Summer's mother's excuse? And what was Damien's role in all this?

Abi could feel herself getting angry but she couldn't lose her temper. That wasn't going to help Summer.

She was completely out of her depth, maybe a change of topic would work best she thought as she launched into a discussion about what breed of dog would suit Summer best. Abi had no idea what Damien's thoughts were on dog ownership but right now she didn't care. If he got asked a few curly questions about getting a puppy, that wasn't her problem. The way she saw it, he owed her a favour or two after today.

Summer was lying on the floor, playing with Jonty, when Abi heard Damien's car pull into her driveway. She went out onto the first-floor deck to direct him up-stairs. The moment she heard his voice Summer jumped up from the floor and threw herself into her father's arms, and narrowly avoided crushing a bunch of irises that Damien clutched in his hands.

'Daddy, Daddy, Abi has a dog. Come and see.'

'Hang on one second, gorgeous girl, I need to put these down first.'

He lowered Summer to the floor and handed the irises to Abi. 'These are for you,' he said.

'What for?' Abi asked.

'To say thank you.'

'You didn't need to do that.'

'Yes, I did,' he insisted. 'You saved my bacon and I didn't want you to think I didn't appreciate it.'

Her apartment was small and Damien was stand-ing awfully close to her. He smelt fresh and clean—he must have showered quickly after surgery—and his proximity was making her flustered. She was far too aware of him.

'I'll just put these into a vase,' she said, inventing a reason to move away from him. She stepped backwards into her narrow galley kitchen that ran along the back wall of the living space and separated her bedroom from the rest of the apartment. She opened a couple of cup-boards hopefully. She didn't think she actually owned a vase. She'd never needed one, no one had ever given her flowers before. Her ex-boyfriend, Mark, had showered her with expensive jewellery that had never really suited her—she'd always felt it had been too sophisticated or mature for her—and looking now at this simple bunch of irises she knew which gift she preferred.

At the back of one of the cupboards she found an old china jug that she assumed belonged to Irma. That would do. She filled it with water, arranged the flowers in it and displayed them on the kitchen counter. The irises were a rich, deep blue with yellow centres and looked surprisingly cheery on the bench. She'd never put much store in the power of a bunch of beautiful flowers but that was because she'd never received any. Being given flowers was so much nicer than picking up a bunch at the weekend market for herself. It shouldn't make any difference, especially given the circumstances, but Abi was touched by Damien's gesture.

She swallowed hard to dislodge the lump that had formed in her throat as Damien pulled out one of the stools at her kitchen counter and took a seat. Abi stayed on the opposite side of the bench, a safe distance away.

'Dad, can we have pizza for dinner?' Summer climbed up onto the stool next to Damien and Abi was struck again by the strong family resemblance now that they were side by side.

'I'll pick one up on the way home.'

'I want to go out for pizza and I want Abi and Jonty to come.'

'Would you like to come with us?' Damien asked her. 'My shout.'

Abi shook her head. 'No, thank you.' She really wasn't up to going out. She'd had enough stressful situations to cope with today and, while sharing a pizza with Damien and Summer sounded appealing, tackling another unknown and unsecured location didn't.

'Please come, Abi, please.' Summer was begging but Abi couldn't do it.

'Sorry, you've probably already got plans,' Damien said, misunderstanding her refusal of his invitation. 'We've taken up enough of your time, we'll get going. Summer, get your things and say goodbye, please.'

'No, it's not that,' Abi said. She didn't want to be alone. She knew the house was going to feel quiet and empty when they left. 'I don't want to leave Jonty,' she told him. 'What about if we got pizza delivered?'

'Are you sure?' Damien asked, as Summer jumped about excitedly, happy to have had her wish granted.

Abi nodded. 'Positive.'

'It's still my shout,' he said, as Summer returned to Jonty's side and Abi pulled a delivery menu off the fridge.

She wasn't about to argue and as she phoned their order through Damien added, 'I'm not sure if I should be letting Summer get away with it. I'm sure she's milking the fact that I didn't pick her up from school. She's playing on my guilt.'

'Really?' Abi wasn't so sure. 'She can manipulate you like that at her age?'

'You'd better believe it. She knows exactly how to play me. I think she gets that from her mother. She's an actress and Summer has definitely inherited the dramatic gene from her.'

'She's an actress?'

'Yes. And quite a good one.'

'Is that why she's gone to New York?' Presented with the opportunity, Abi couldn't resist asking some questions but she busied herself looking for napkins and plates so that Damien hopefully didn't feel as though he was being interrogated.

Damien was nodding. 'She got called in for an audition for a television series and, as usual, she didn't worry about any pre-existing commitments, just dropped everything and went.'

'Have you heard from her?'

'Not directly. There was a message on my phone, asking me to collect Summer, but of course I was in Theatre so I didn't see it. She's never understood that I can't monitor my emails or even check my phone constantly throughout the day. Brooke exists in her own world and has never made an attempt to put herself in someone else's shoes. This isn't the first time she's changed plans without consulting me, but her world is all about her and she refuses to consider others, even her own daughter.'

Abi felt her sympathy for Summer strengthen. She knew what it was like to have a mother who did not have her children as a priority. Whether it was because they couldn't or wouldn't cope wasn't the point. Either way it left the children feeling neglected and unloved and that was no way for any child to grow up.

'Did she say when she'd be back?'

'No. She wouldn't consider that I would need to know that.'

'But what about Summer?'

'Brooke will expect me to handle it.'

Abi found the whole situation incredible. It was obvious that Damien and Brooke had some issues with their channels of communication but that wasn't really any of her business—unless Damien made it a habit to involve her. At this stage she couldn't get involved but that didn't stop her from wanting to know more about their situation. She knew she shouldn't care but Summer was so sweet and Damien was so gorgeous and she had to admit she was wondering what sort of woman would catch his eye. If Summer's mother was an actress she was probably beautiful. There must be something special about her if Damien was letting her get away with treating him so disrespectfully, but in Abi's eyes that didn't excuse her behaviour, particularly towards Summer. Damien said it wasn't the first time Summer hadn't been collected. Why did he let her get away with it?

Damien had only talked about 'Summer's mother', he hadn't mentioned a wife. Were they divorced? Never married? What was the state of their relationship? Now and previously. Abi's curiosity was piqued but she couldn't ask those questions.

'You didn't ask?' Abi wanted to know more but Damien wasn't answering. He was watching Summer and Abi guessed he didn't want the conversation to be overheard.

'Summer, would you like to brush Jonty while we wait for our pizza?' she suggested, knowing that Summer wouldn't refuse.

'She's been asking for a dog but I really don't think we have the time to devote to one,' Damien said as his daughter headed downstairs to the utility room to look for Jonty's brush.

'I know. She told me,' Abi replied.

Damien shot a glance Abi's way, a worried look in his dark eyes. 'What else did she tell you?'

'Actually, she did tell me one thing that I think you should hear.' Abi moved around the kitchen bench to take a seat at the counter beside Damien. She needed to tell him what Summer had said but she felt she needed to be closer. What she was about to say felt a bit like spilling a secret and she couldn't do it from across the kitchen bench. It needed to be said quietly, as if saying it loudly would make it real. Although Abi had a suspicion that what Summer had told her was true.

'She told me that her mother didn't want her.' Even repeating Summer's words made Abi's heart ache and seeing Damien's expression just made it worse. He looked sad and resigned but not surprised, and Abi realised that her suspicion was correct. Summer had been telling the truth.

Damien was nodding his head. 'I know. Brooke never made any secret of the fact that her career was going to come before anything else and we weren't planning on having kids when she fell pregnant, but I always hoped that she'd embrace motherhood once the baby arrived. But Brooke has never bonded with Summer. She enjoys dressing her up and taking her out but she seems to think of her as an accessory rather than her daughter. A child takes a lot of time and energy and Brooke prefers to spend that time and energy on herself. I knew she didn't want children but I still can't believe that she's told Summer that.'

In Abi's opinion Brooke sounded nothing like the kind of woman she imagined Damien to have chosen.

'What if she gets this job in New York?'

Damien shrugged. 'I'll worry about that then.'

He tried to sound relaxed and unconcerned but the reality was the idea terrified him. If Brooke got the offer of a permanent gig on the other side of the country, how would that affect him and, more importantly, Summer?

But Abi voiced his concern. 'What if she wants to take Summer?'

'I can't imagine she'd want to do that. She really doesn't have one maternal bone in her body.' That had become perfectly clear in the demise of their marriage. 'She has no time for Summer and Summer is definitely not Brooke's priority. Unfortunately she doesn't even try to pretend otherwise. But I will always do what's best for Summer and I would fight tooth and nail to keep her with me.'

Damien hated the fact that he'd been unable to make his marriage work. He hated being a failure, even though he knew that he and Brooke were both to blame. But it was irrelevant now. Marriage was not something he intended to try again. His focus was elsewhere. Summer was his number one priority, followed by his career.

Summer was yawning as Damien finished off the last slice of pizza. He wiped his hands on his napkin and said, 'It's getting late. We'd better go.'

Abi and Damien stood up from the kitchen bench at the same time. They were inches apart and Abi could feel the air crackling around them, surrounding them in a field of electricity.

She could feel herself being drawn in by his eyes, so dark it was impossible to fathom what was going on behind them. She could see the shadow of the day's growth of his beard, dark on his jaw and chin, and along with the strong straight line of his nose there was something totally masculine about him. He looked powerful yet she'd seen how gentle and kind he was with Summer. He projected strength but also sensitivity and he was utterly gorgeous to boot.

She forgot all her rules, all her reasons why she was single and staying that way. Damien had captured her imagination and she wanted to know more about him. Where he had come from, why he had married, what had attracted him to his wife and what was the state of his relationship with her. She wanted to know what he tasted like. What he felt like and what it would feel like to have his lips brush across hers.

She could feel herself leaning towards him. Perhaps the field was magnetic, not electric, but it was almost too powerful to resist. Was it her imagination or was he leaning towards her too?

Abi felt pressure against her leg, a knock, a bump. She looked down. Summer had squeezed herself between them and wrapped herself around Damien's leg, breaking the spell, releasing the tension that surrounded them.

Damien bent down, scooped his daughter into his arms and stepped back. He picked up her school bag and Abi stood at the top of the stairs and watched them leave. She had to force herself not to follow.

What would that achieve? Why would she want to?

She had to keep her distance. Yes, he was an attractive man, gorgeous even, and he was wonderful with Summer, but he was also a colleague and she couldn't go there again. This time she knew his life was complicated. This time she would have no excuses. It sounded as though his relationship with Summer's mother was extremely difficult and she had vowed that her next relationship would be simple, straightforward. Next time she was going in with her eyes open.

Next time! Next relationship! Why was she even thinking like that? She was in no hurry to go there again and when she was ready a man like Damien would not be on her list. A complicated man with baggage who she also had to work with—she couldn't afford to even think about that.

CHAPTER FOUR

THERE WAS A light knock on Damien's open office door and he looked up in anticipation, hoping to see Abi. Disappointment lodged in the back of his throat when he saw Freya standing there instead. He should have known it wasn't Abi as her scent, already familiar to him, always preceded her.

She smelt of fresh peaches and sunshine, she smelt like the month of July, of summer, and her amber eyes blazed with warmth in contrast to her cool, pale skin. He wondered if she tasted of peaches as well and for a moment last night he'd thought about finding out. He'd been tempted to kiss her. Caught up in a moment of madness, he'd been tempted to press his lips to hers and taste her.

For one crazy moment he'd forgotten about his daughter, he'd forgotten about his issues with his ex-wife—all he'd been aware of was Abi. He'd been drawn to her. There was something between them, a connection that he hadn't felt with anyone for a long time. He didn't think he was imagining it, he was certain she felt it too. He was certain he'd seen desire in her golden eyes and he'd definitely seen her lean towards him—or had he leaned towards her?—but then reality had forced its way between them in the form of an impatient five-year-old. Although that was probably just as well. He couldn't jump in, despite wanting to. All his energy was directed at his work and his daughter, and he had no room in his life for anything else.

But he couldn't keep thoughts of Abi out of his head. So much about her was already familiar and he was still trying to process how that could be after only a few days. How was it that she had worked her way into his subconscious so swiftly? There was something ethereal and mystical about her. She was weaving her magic over him, casting a spell.

'Are you okay?' Freya asked, and Damien was aware only then that his thoughts were drifting.

He shook his head to clear it. 'Yes, I'm fine. What can I do for you?'

'I just wanted to check on how Abi's first day went. Did you have any problems? Is there anything I need to know about?'

'No, everything's good.' Everything except his equilibrium but that wasn't Freya's department.

'What do you think of her?'

'Is this where you want me to say, "You were right"?' he asked, but Freya didn't reply, just smiled at him and raised an eyebrow. Damien decided he wasn't going to give her the satisfaction of the truth. 'You chose well, she's extremely competent,' he said.

'Oh, I know that,' Freya responded. 'I meant what do you think of her as a person? She's cute, isn't she?'

'I hadn't noticed,' he lied. He didn't want to notice cute women. He had enough going on in his life without complicating things by adding women into the mix. But his brain was defying instructions and he was spending far too much time contemplating Abi Thompson. He couldn't admit the truth, not to Freya. He knew she would want to meddle. She was happy in her new relationship with Zack and Damien knew she thought everyone around her should be so lucky. He didn't need her interference.

'Really?'

'Really.'

He was happy on his own. He didn't need, or want, a woman at this point in his life. He'd made a mess of his marriage and he knew it had made him gun-shy. He'd got so many things wrong, starting with his judgement of Brooke's character. He'd been badly burned and he hated the knowledge that his marriage had failed; he hated not making a success of things. His focus now was on his daughter and that was how things should be. That was how things had to be.

'So, if you'll excuse me I have a meeting with Mila shortly and I need to get a few things ready.'

Freya didn't argue but she did give him a look that implied she hadn't believed a word he'd said. That didn't bother him. She could believe what she liked. It didn't mean she was right.

Abi had struggled to get out of bed that morning. She'd lain awake for hours, tossing and turning, willing herself to sleep, but her mind had been buzzing with thoughts of Damien. When she had slept she'd been so wired that the extra adrenalin had given nightmares permission to intensify. Several times she'd been woken by dreams that had seemed even more vivid and real and dreadful than normal. She'd thought she was getting used to these dreams, she thought she'd learned what to expect, but last night had been particularly horrific and she was exhausted as a consequence.

When she arrived at the office, bleary-eyed and fuzzy-headed, she was informed by Jennifer that her day's schedule had been slightly revised and Damien wanted to see her.

Walking into his office, Abi saw a very attractive woman sitting in the chair by the window. In the chair Abi had sat in just yesterday. She stood as Abi entered the room.

She was about Abi's height with hazel eyes and amazing hair, thick, long and dark with mahogany high-lights. She looked very 'together', sensible, calm, un-flustered, serene and rich. She looked like old money and Abi fancied that she even smelt like money.

Damien looked as neat and tidy as always and the two of them made a striking pair.

'This is Dr Mila Brightman from the Bright Hope Clinic,' Damien introduced her. 'Do you remember I mentioned the joint venture that Freya has been work-ing on?' he said as Mila shook Abi's hand.

Abi nodded. Freya had also talked about this and she remembered some basic information. The Bright Hope Clinic was located in Southern LA, demographi-cally an area that was the polar opposite of The Holly-wood Hills. It had been established to provide medical services to underprivileged children, both in LA and abroad, and Freya had recently established a project allowing the Bright Hope Clinic to access The Hills' facilities and staff on a pro bono basis. The first joint patient had been operated on just recently, a little boy who had undergone complicated heart surgery. Abi had heard all about Paulo and the success of the surgery.

Freya had been hugely excited and was planning a function to celebrate the partnership between the clinics and to garner some good publicity. She intended to promote The Hills and attract sponsorship for the Bright Hope Clinic at the same time.

'I heard about Paulo. That was quite a success story,' she commented, but she didn't mention the forthcoming party—she had no intention of attending that if she could possibly avoid it.

Mila was beaming. 'It was incredible! He is an amazing little boy with quite a spark, and to have such a great result was brilliant. You know no one expected him to survive the surgery? No one would touch him and to think he not only survived but is thriving is fantastic. Just imagine the amazing things we might be able to achieve together.'

'The Bright Hope Clinic is Mila's project,' Damien explained. 'She established it, it's her baby, and she has another patient who needs our assistance.'

Abi was keen to hear more.

'I was hoping you could help,' Mila said, as Abi took a seat. 'Damien tells me you've had a lot of experience with burns victims?'

'Unfortunately, yes. In Afghanistan.'

'We have a patient, a seven-year-old boy with third-degree burns to his arms and chest, sustained in a house fire. Dylan tried to put the fire out but was trapped and received extensive burns before the fire brigade could retrieve him.'

'When did this happen?'

'Four days ago. His mother was referred to us with an enquiry about skin-graft surgery. They don't have any medical insurance but I don't have any doctors who are skilled in this area. I am hoping that it is something you might be able to do here.'

From what Abi had been briefly told this would be exactly the type of case that Freya was keen to support and Abi was happy to help if she could. 'I've had lots of experience with burns victims but they've been adults,' she told Mila.

'The principle is the same surely?'

Abi nodded. The only issue she could envisage was dependent on the size of the area that needed grafts and whether or not a seven-year-old would have enough skin for donation, but she wouldn't know that until she'd examined the patient. 'When can I see him?' she asked.

Damien answered. 'He's being transferred by ambulance as we speak,' he said.

Abi looked at him quizzically and he shrugged his shoulders in reply. His tailored jacket lifted and then fell again to hang perfectly from his broad shoulders. 'I thought it might be a case you'd be interested in taking on,' he explained. 'It's not cosmetic surgery. As such, it's more along your lines, and I was pretty sure you'd agree to Mila's proposal.' He smiled at her and she knew that he wouldn't have much trouble getting her to agree to a good number of things.

But he was right. She'd enjoyed being in Theatre yesterday but this type of case, as opposed to cosmetic surgery, was exactly what she would prefer to be doing. A successful outcome would not only be a huge thing for the patient but it would cement her place at The Hills. It would be a challenge but one she was ready for. But she wasn't going to commit that easily and certainly not just because he'd smiled at her.

'I need to assess him first. I need to see whether there is anything I can do before I agree to take him on.'

'Of course,' Mila said as she stood. 'A consultation is all I'm asking for at this stage. Shall we go and meet the ambulance?'

Abi and Mila left Damien's office together, leaving him behind. That was a good thing. She needed to focus, to concentrate on this new case and if Damien had chosen to come with them she knew he would only distract her. But she would swear she could feel his dark-eyed gaze following her out of the room, although she knew she was being completely fanciful. Why would he follow her movements when he could watch Mila instead? Mila was far more glamorous.

'Thank you for agreeing to see Dylan,' Mila said as they stepped into the main corridor and headed for the ambulance bay. 'My clinic is important to me. I want to be able to provide medical care for people who can't afford it but it's an expensive exercise and there will always be some things we just can't do, but with Freya's help and with the support of The Hills we will be able to achieve more.'

Mila might come from a wealthier background than her but Abi sensed that despite that difference they had one thing in common—wanting the best for their patients. It was a common thread among those in the medical profession—patients came first—and Abi had seen it already at The Hills.

As they headed for the ambulance bay Abi could see James Rothsberg—head of The Hills and also Freya's brother and Abi's new boss—walking towards them. Abi felt Mila tense at her side as he approached them and Mila's pace slowed, not enough to stop her movement altogether but Abi got the sense that if the corridor hadn't been long and straight but had presented Mila with an alternate route to take, she would have taken it. She got the feeling that Mila was looking for an escape.

Abi saw James's eyes widen in surprise as they approached him and he stopped short a few steps before he reached them.

'Mila! What are you doing here?' He looked uncomfortable and appeared to be unsure how to greet her. He didn't seem to notice Abi at all. He certainly didn't acknowledge her, having eyes for Mila only.

'I needed to discuss a patient,' she said, as Abi tried to blend into the background. 'I have another patient that I'm hoping can use your services.'

'Already?'

Abi could hear the note of surprise in James's voice, or was it cynicism?

Mila obviously heard it too as her reply was frosty. 'I wasn't aware there was a time limit. Freya assured me you were okay with the collaboration.'

'Of course.'

He didn't sound okay. Abi could sense the tension between them. It was almost palpable and Abi could visualise the sparks snapping backwards and forwards between them. She wondered if she should give them some privacy but she was expecting the ambulance to arrive at any moment with Dylan, and she wanted Mila with her when they greeted their young patient.

In her peripheral vision she saw an ambulance pulling to a stop. James saw it too.

'Well, I guess I'll leave you to it,' he said as he stepped away. 'It was good to see you,' he added, but Abi wasn't at all sure that he meant it.

Mila also seemed a bit unsettled and looked a little lost when James walked away. She was no longer quite so unflustered and serene. Abi wondered what the story was—she was positive there was one.

Mila was still watching as James walked away. The rear doors of the ambulance were being opened and Abi started to move towards the exit. Her movement drew Mila's attention back to the matter at hand and Abi forgot all about Damien and the Bright Hope Clinic and the tension between Mila and James as she focused on her young patient.

'How did Dylan's skin grafts go?' Damien asked as he stuck his head into Abi's office.

Abi had performed the surgery the previous day but this was the first chance Damien had had to follow up the case with her. She swivelled her chair around to face him and stretched her legs out. She was wearing one of The Hills' white coats over a cream silky blouse and a black skirt that finished just above her knees. Her legs were amazing and Damien had to remind himself to keep his eyes fixed on her face and not to ogle her slim calves.

'The procedure went well. Now it's just a matter of waiting to see if the grafts take and keeping my fingers crossed that Dylan doesn't get an infection.'

She looked pleased with herself and so she should. Mila had observed the surgery and Damien had heard from her how impressed she had been with Abi's ability. It seemed as though Freya's decision to offer Abi a position at The Hills had been a good one. She was a competent surgeon, more than competent, and he was enjoying the development of their professional relationship, but he couldn't pretend he hadn't noticed her other attributes. She was beautiful in a fragile, delicate way but he sensed an underlying strength and he was keen to find out more about her, which brought him to the other reason for his visit.

Freya's party was only a day away but, according to Freya, Abi was making excuses to avoid attending Saturday night's function. Damien hadn't been particularly keen on attending either but when Freya had made it clear that she expected all senior staff to make an appearance at the publicity event he'd decided that one way to make the evening more appealing would be to have Abi there too.

He knew he should attend, it could be good for business, but since he and Brooke had split he'd avoided as many of these social gatherings as he could. He'd had enough of dressing up and parading around and chatting to people who didn't really interest him. He much preferred to spend his weekend nights lying on the couch, watching a movie and sharing a bowl of popcorn with Summer.

But that revelation had given him a brief glimpse into the future and he hadn't liked what he'd seen. He was in danger of becoming a sad, lonely old man. While, if anyone asked, he would tell them he wasn't interested in dating he didn't really want to end up old and alone. Summer wouldn't be with him for ever and he knew he should make more of an effort but there wasn't normally much incentive to do so. Women were trouble. Until now.

Until Abi had come into his world he would have been quite happy to remain a hermit but now the thought of being able to escort her to the function appealed to him and therefore so did the function. Now he had some incentive.

'Dylan's case was an interesting one for you?' he asked, posing the question while he tried to think of a way to segue into his proposition.

She nodded and her unusual amber eyes glowed.

'Do you feel like celebrating a successful first week on the job?' he asked.

'I won't know how successful I've been until Dylan's bandages come off next week.'

'Freya has organised this cocktail party for tomorrow night. It's part promotion, part celebration and we are all expected to attend, but I'd rather poke myself in the eye with a sharp stick. She tells me you feel much the same.'

Abi nodded. 'Having to mingle with a room full of strangers is my idea of purgatory,' she said.

'In that case, I have a suggestion.' He took a deep breath as an unfamiliar burst of nerves made his heart jump in his chest. 'Seeing as this party is supposed to be spotlighting the joint venture between The Hills and the Bright Hope Clinic and you've just had your very first joint-venture patient, I think that if I have to go, you should come with me.' He shouldn't be doing this but he was. He wanted to find out what made her tick. She was intriguing, a mixture of strength and fragility, a complicated combination—her army background combined with her delicate looks. Was she made of steel or spun silk like a spider web? Whichever it was, a mesh or a web, he was ensnared. 'I'll pick you up and I promise we'll just make a brief appearance and then we can escape. I'm going to use the babysitter excuse.'

'You have an excuse worked out already?'

'It pays to be prepared.' He grinned and was relieved to see an answering smile from Abi. 'And if you let me give you a lift, you'll have an excuse to leave too.'

She laughed and Damien felt the warm glow spread further through his body. He hadn't heard her laugh before and the sound burst from her, rich and joyous and completely unexpected. She sounded confident and full of life. Her laugh had wiped out all traces of fragility, leaving a sense of excitement and anticipation, and he knew he was going to do everything he could to make her laugh again.

'I've run out of excuses,' she said once she stopped laughing. 'I even tried telling Freya I have nothing to wear but then she offered to lend me a dress. So I think I will use your excuse. I would love a lift, thank you.'

Abi hesitated in the entrance and fiddled with the small diamond studs in her ears. She had sold all the jewellery Mark had given her during their ill-fated relationship when she'd discovered his deception. She'd only ever liked it because he'd given it to her but it hadn't really been her style— it was too ostentatious for her. She had simpler tastes and once she'd discovered the truth about Mark the jewellery had made her feel cheap and naive. She'd used the proceeds to buy herself a simple pair of diamond studs. They were the only decent jewellery she owned.

'Are you coming in?' Damien asked.

She hadn't been sure if accepting Damien's offer of a lift had been a wise decision. She still wasn't sure but after discussing the facts with her psychologist she had decided not to rescind his invitation. Caroline had convinced her that she needed to start socialising and she had suggested that this cocktail event would provide a perfect opportunity. It was in a safe, familiar location with a large number of people she already knew and there was no need for her to stay for hours. She could make an appearance and once she'd had enough she could leave. Abi wasn't totally convinced but she had agreed to give it a go, though she had known she wouldn't have the courage to arrive on her own. Damien's invitation had seemed like the lesser of two evils.

'Shall we?' Damien asked.

He was still waiting patiently for her. She needed to get moving, they couldn't stand outside all night. She ran her hands down the front of her dress, Freya's dress, in a self-conscious, nervous gesture.

'Don't worry, you look gorgeous,' he said.

'Really?'

Abi had been worried about this dress. She'd never owned or worn anything like it but she had no option. It was a simple sheath with thin spaghetti straps but its simplicity belied its eye-catching silhouette. The dress was made of gold sequins that matched her eyes and it shimmered and sparkled as she moved. It looked expensive and it was. There would be no hiding in the corner in this one. She had draped a black wrap over her shoulders in an attempt to tone the outfit down but she still felt very conspicuous. 'I was worried it might be too much. It's not too revealing?'

Damien shook his head. 'It's perfect.'

'Thank you.' His compliment sent a thrill of pleasure through her and boosted her confidence. She wanted to tell him that he looked amazing too but she couldn't summon the courage. He was in a black evening suit,

single breasted, cut to his slim frame, drawing attention to the blackness of his hair and eyes. She wasn't
a girl who was taken in by a man in uniform, years of
army life had made her immune to that, but a man in
a dinner suit with a crisp white shirt and a bow tie that
had been tied on, not clipped, was a different story.
Especially when it was carried off as well as Damien
did. He could have stepped off the cover of a magazine.

He placed a hand in the small of her back and ushered her towards the door. A security guard was sta-
tioned there and Abi felt herself relax, knowing no
unexpected guests would have gained entry.

Together they stepped into the clinic foyer, where
Abi stopped and looked around her in awe. The foyer
was normally spectacular, reminding her of a modern
art gallery, but Freya had outdone herself tonight. Chandeliers had been hung from the ceiling, enormous crys-
tal vases held oversized flower arrangements, a string
quartet played in the corner and young, beautiful wait-
ers, whom Abi suspected would be models or actors,
served French champagne.

The party spilled from the reception area into the
internal courtyard, although the room was not yet
crowded. Abi was relieved to see that she and Damien
were among the first to arrive. She wasn't brave enough
to walk into a room full of people, it was far better if
the room filled up around her.

Freya had timed the party to begin at sunset and
the view of the city sparkling below them as the lights
began to come on was spectacular. Freya was greeting
guests just inside the door. Abi knew it wasn't tech-
nically Freya's party but that was how she thought of
it. She had talked of nothing but work and the party

all week and even though the party was a publicity event for The Hills and for the Bright Hope Clinic, Abi couldn't help but associate it with Freya.

Even the guests looked as if they could all be Freya's friends. Everyone looked rich—some looked like new money, others like old, but Abi was neither. She had grown up poor, something she doubted any of these people were familiar with. Although she looked the part tonight she still felt a great divide between her and everyone else. There wasn't anything she could do about it but she didn't like it and she worried that the guests would see through her smoke-and-mirrors dress to the girl who had grown up poor, raised by an alcoholic single mother.

'Abi, let me check your wrap.' Damien's voice interrupted her thoughts. His hands were on her arms and she could feel the warmth of his fingers spreading through her body as he started to slip the wrap from her shoulders.

She wanted to go with him to the coat check. She didn't want to wander unaccompanied among the other guests, and she didn't want to introduce herself to strangers. She was about to follow him when Mila appeared by her side.

'Good, you're here,' Mila greeted her. 'Come with me, there's someone I want you to meet.'

'I'll catch up with you later,' Damien said, as Mila tucked her arm into Abi's almost as if she was afraid Abi would run away if she didn't keep hold of her.

As Mila led her through the crowd Abi felt as though she'd been dropped into a movie set, a glamorous, old-school Hollywood movie. It was good in a way as it didn't feel like real life. Perhaps if she could pretend it was make-believe she would be able to relax and enjoy the evening.

Mila stopped next to a solid, muscular man with cropped dirty blond hair and brown eyes and introduced her. 'Here she is. Abi, this is Tyler Richardson, my boyfriend.'

Abi was taken by surprise. After witnessing the exchange, and the tension, between Mila and James earlier in the week she realised she hadn't expected Mila to have a boyfriend. Maybe Tyler was the source of the tension she had felt.

'It's good to meet you.' Tyler took her hand and shook it hard. He seemed laid back and relaxed but she couldn't figure out why he'd want to meet her. 'I wanted to thank you,' he continued.

'Thank me? For what?'

'For taking on Dylan's care.'

Abi frowned, unsure what connection Tyler had with her patient.

'I'm a fireman,' he explained, as Mila excused herself to visit the bathroom. 'I was in the crew that went to the scene of Dylan's accident. I pulled him out of the house.'

'Oh, I see. Is that how he ended up at the Bright Hope Clinic? Through you?'

'I called in at the hospital to see how he was doing and spoke to his mum and mentioned that Mila's clinic might be able to help. How did the surgery go? How is he?'

'I'm not sure how much I can tell you without breaking confidentiality,' Abi replied.

'That's okay. It's just that when we are able to save someone it's nice to know how they're doing. Sometimes we never hear anything. We rescue someone and then...' he spread his hands wide '...nothing. The nurses in the public hospitals will often give us a bit of an update. Hearing that someone survived and is doing well helps make our job worthwhile, it helps to make up for the ones that don't go so well. But once he was moved out of there it was almost impossible to find out anything.'

Abi could understand that. Tyler wasn't so different from her, trying to make a difference, trying to save lives. Hearing good news always lifted spirits. What could she tell him? She was happy with Dylan's progress but it was early days. The bandages wouldn't be removed for another couple of days so it was impossible to tell how successful the grafts had been. The only positives at this stage were that she'd been able to do the grafts and that Dylan's temperature was normal, indicating the absence of infection. She compromised. 'It's still early but I'm happy at this point. He'll be with us for another week. Do you want me to ask his mum if you can visit?'

Tyler nodded. 'I'd like that, thank you.'

Abi smiled at him. She knew exactly where he stood, and she was still smiling when James approached them.

James Rothsberg was a handsome man, tall and fair-haired with blue eyes and great bone structure—Abi always noticed bone structure, she was trained to do that—but although he was good-looking and of a similar build to Damien, he wasn't nearly as striking. Damien was sleeker and leaner but their contrasting colouring made her think of positives and negatives, and Damien was the positive. She couldn't ignore Damien and even now her eyes searched the crowd, looking for his familiar figure. There was something about Damien that captured her attention, something that went beyond the fact that he was tall, dark and handsome. She'd have to be careful and keep her guard up around him if she didn't want to make a fool of herself.

'Abi, one week gone. How are you settling in?' her new boss asked.

'More smoothly than I expected,' she said. She'd been busy. The film industry awards were a week away, which had bolstered her patient list, and Dylan's case had kept her on her toes, but she'd enjoyed her first week.

But James barely listened to her reply before offering his hand to Tyler. It seemed she wasn't the only one whose mind was wandering.

'Did you come with Abi?' he asked Tyler.

'No, Tyler is with me.' Mila had reappeared and answered before Tyler had a chance.

Abi could tell from James's expression that Mila's answer wasn't the one he'd been hoping for. Although the air around them was chilly at the moment, it was obvious that at some point these two had been more than acquaintances.

James made polite small talk for a few minutes but Abi noticed that when Mila headed to the opposite end of the room to prepare for the speeches, James's eyes followed her.

The string quartet finished their set and lapsed into silence as Mila and Freya stepped up onto a raised platform that had been positioned in front of the reception desk. As the speeches began Abi felt Damien's presence at her side. The air stirred whenever he was near;

it seemed to move differently around him. She turned to her right.

'Are you okay?' he asked. 'Having a good time?'

She wasn't really. She still felt uncomfortable and out of place, although she was better when Damien was near. Her world seemed to make more sense and her doubts and fears lessened, even though she still felt off balance, but she knew that was because of the effect he had on her rather than her own uncertainties and insecurities. But she nodded, trying to project confidence as she listened to the speeches.

Mila took the microphone first. She spoke passionately about the aims of the Bright Hope Clinic and about Paulo, who had been the first joint-venture patient between the two clinics. After the success of the first operation Freya had plans to ramp up the cooperation between the two clinics but she needed funding. Her speech emphasised the success of the first surgery and encouraged the wealthy LA guests to contribute to the charitable organisation she and James were establishing. That would give Mila access to the funds she needed, as well as bring good publicity for The Hills.

Both of them spoke very well about their vision for the partnership but Abi knew it was easy to talk in public when you were invested in and knowledgeable about your topic, and while she was interested in the project she could listen to Freya without watching. There were other things that had caught her attention, like what was going on between Mila and James. James's eyes were still glued to Mila. It was easy to see why, she was a beautiful woman, but Abi could feel that it was more than that.

'Ready to go?' Damien asked, as the speeches wrapped up.

He had his car keys in his hand. Abi could hear them jingling in his fist. They had agreed to leave as soon as possible after the speeches. Abi had known she would have had enough of the crowd by then, and Damien wanted to get home at a reasonable time to relieve the babysitter. Abi also wanted to get home to Jonty. Irma and George were away for the weekend, visiting their daughter, so Jonty was home alone.

She nodded. 'Give me a minute to grab my wrap.'

'I'll get it for you, I have the ticket.' Damien pulled the stub from his pocket. The storeroom behind the reception desk had been doing double duty as a coat check for the evening, manned by their regular receptionist, Stephanie, and Abi could see James making his way towards the desk and to Mila, who had just stepped off the platform at the conclusion of the speeches.

Curiosity got the better of her. 'It's okay,' she said as she took the ticket from his fingers. 'I'll only be a second.' She wanted another opportunity to examine Mila and James.

She headed for the coat check. James and Mila stood at one end of the reception desk, looking tense. Freya had disappeared into the crowd before James had crossed the room, leaving Mila and James alone. Not wanting to disturb them, she approached the desk from the opposite end but their conversation carried to her.

'Mila, can I talk to you?' James reached out a hand but Mila stepped back.

'It's not really a good time,' she replied, and again Abi got the sense that if there was somewhere that Mila could run and hide she would do so.

Abi handed Stephanie her ticket. She kept her face averted from Mila and James as she waited for Stephanie to fetch her wrap but it didn't stop her from being able to overhear their conversation. She didn't like to think of it as eavesdropping but she was fascinated by the tension between them.

'I'm sorry for everything,' James said, but he didn't elaborate on what 'everything' was and Mila didn't question him; she obviously knew what he was talking about.

'You want to apologise but you don't want to explain?' she said.

'I can't.'

'Can't or won't?'

Mila waited for an answer but James was mute. Stephanie returned with Abi's wrap as Mila said, 'It doesn't matter any more anyway. It's ancient history.' She brushed past James as she added, 'Tyler is waiting for me. I have to go.'

Mila's path took her within a couple of feet of Abi but she didn't look at her. Abi thought she could see tears in her eyes.

Abi glanced at James. She couldn't help herself. She wanted to see his reaction. He wasn't looking at her either so Abi followed the line of his gaze. His eyes were on Tyler, who was on the other side of the room, chatting with Freya's boyfriend, Zack. It didn't look as if Tyler was waiting for Mila. Why had she made that excuse? And what was James apologising for? There was definite history between them but from James's expression Abi was guessing that he didn't want it to be history. He'd looked jealous.

'Do you know if everything is okay between Mila

and James?' she couldn't resist asking Damien as she sank into the soft leather of his car seat as he wound his way down through the Hollywood Hills and back to Pacific Palisades.

'Mila and *James*?' he queried. 'Why?'

'There just seemed to be a bit of tension between them and I wondered what it was all about. Whether there is an issue with the joint venture?' She added a reason in case Damien thought she was being too inquisitive.

'The joint venture was Freya's idea but as far as I know James is behind it. They're both very conscious of giving back to the community, even though Freya is the one driving it. I'm not aware of any issues.'

That didn't mean there weren't issues, it just meant that, as a man, Damien possibly hadn't noticed anything.

But her own fabricated question made her wonder if she was mistaken. Perhaps it was simply a conflict over the joint venture. Perhaps it wasn't jealousy but a financial issue. Not love but money?

Damien pulled into her driveway and as he killed the engine Abi could hear Jonty barking. She frowned. He wasn't a noisy dog usually. He hadn't barked when she'd come home from work this week but then he'd had George and Irma there. Perhaps he recognised the sound of Damien's car and was excited to think he finally had company.

'Is that Jonty?' Damien asked, as he got out of the car and came around to open Abi's door.

Abi nodded and as she stepped out onto the driveway Jonty came tearing around the corner of the converted garage and skidded to a halt by her side.

Abi scratched behind his ears. 'Hello, boy. What's got into you? Did you miss me?'

Damien walked Abi around to her door which was on the side of the garage and opened up to lead onto the internal stairway. Jonty was barking again as Abi pulled her keys from her handbag. 'Shush,' she said as she pushed the doggy door with her foot, thinking that perhaps once Jonty was inside he'd stop barking, but the doggy door didn't swing open.

'That's strange,' she said.

'What is?'

'The doggy door is locked. I'm certain I wouldn't have locked him out.' Jonty had stopped barking but he was pacing and whining at her feet as she slid her key into the lock.

'Wait.' Damien put his hand on her wrist and her skin thrummed with the heat of his touch. As she turned to look at him she heard a noise upstairs in her apartment. The sound of something falling over.

There was somebody in her apartment.

CHAPTER FIVE

ABI FROZE. SHE COULDN'T have moved if she'd wanted to. This feeling was familiar to her. This sense of feeling helpless, useless and most of all vulnerable. Knowing she should be doing something but unable to make her body function.

Her brain shut down. It was unable to issue instructions. Normally she was a quick, decisive person, years of training in medicine and in the armed forces had instilled that in her, but since returning from Afghanistan she had lost that ability to make a swift decision under pressure, unless it was in a medical context. The slightest bit of stress or anxiety outside work rendered her incapable. And the thought that she was vulnerable in those situations terrified her even more, which only served to worsen her predicament.

Damien showed no such hesitation. He stepped in front of her as she remained standing, rooted to the spot. He unlocked the door and Jonty raced past him as it opened and tore up the stairs, barking madly once more when he was thwarted again by another closed door that led into the apartment.

Damien followed Jonty. He made no attempt to climb the stairs quietly but, Abi supposed, there was no need for stealth. Her dog had well and truly announced their arrival.

He reached for the handle. She wanted to tell him not to open it, to be careful, but the words lodged in her throat and although she opened her mouth she couldn't get the words to come out. Fear rendered her speechless but she had recovered control of her limbs and was able to follow him up the stairs. Even that was driven by fear. She was more afraid of being left alone at the bottom of the stairs than confronting whatever was at the top. She needed to stay close to Damien, even if it meant closing the gap between her and danger.

As he turned the handle and pushed the door open Abi heard the sound of glass breaking. His back blocked her view so she craned her neck and stood on her toes to look past his shoulder, just in time to see a figure disappearing through her balcony doors and onto her deck.

Jonty dashed across the room and Damien followed, crossing the floor in four strides. Abi was close behind him, her heels crunching through the fragments of broken glass that had fallen out of the balcony doors as they had been slammed open and which now lay strewn across the deck.

The balcony was empty. Abi's heart was beating at a million miles an hour but she breathed a sigh of relief when she realised they were too late. She hadn't stopped to think about what might happen if they confronted the intruder but, thank God, they weren't about to find out.

Whoever had been in Abi's house had leapt over the railing of the deck and dropped eight feet to the lawn below. All they saw was a figure in dark clothing land awkwardly and run across George and Irma's lawn at a fast limp.

Damien had both hands on the top of the railing as he watched the retreating figure hobble away. 'He must have twisted his ankle when he landed. Shall I go after him?''

This time it was Abi's hand on Damien's arm as a precautionary gesture. 'No!'

'But I can catch him.'

'And then what? What if he has a knife? Or a gun?' Abi could feel herself shaking as adrenalin flooded her system. Her heart was racing again. She couldn't put Damien in danger. It was better just to let the man go. She wanted to avoid danger and minimise harm at all costs. 'He wouldn't have found anything worth stealing, I have nothing of any value. Let him go, it's not worth the risk.'

Her wrap had slipped off her shoulders and caught in the crook of her elbows and Damien reached over and lifted it back around her. The touch of his fingers made her tremble even more.

'Are you okay?' he asked.

She had no idea.

Damien insisted on checking the rest of the apartment to make sure there was no accomplice and Abi insisted on going with him. Even though her apartment was small with very few hiding places and wouldn't take long to search she didn't want to be left on her own. There was safety in numbers. There was safety with Damien.

She and Jonty followed behind him as he cleared the upstairs, a task that didn't take long as besides the kitchen and living area there was only Abi's bedroom and the bathroom. Coming out of the bathroom, Abi noticed that Jonty was protecting his front paw. She was torn between sticking close to Damien or checking the dog, but once they had finished investigating the upstairs Abi decided to tend to Jonty, letting Damien check the garage and utility room downstairs alone. There had been no more noises. It appeared that the intruder hadn't had company and she felt it was safe to stay upstairs.

She knelt on the kitchen floor and picked a piece of glass from Jonty's paw. It took her a while as her hands were shaking but once she was confident it was out she retrieved some first-aid supplies from the bathroom cabinet and washed his foot clean with antiseptic solution. She didn't bother to bandage it. Now that the glass was out it didn't appear to be worrying him and she knew he'd only gnaw at the bandage until it came off.

Damien reappeared from downstairs. 'There's a broken window in the garage,' he said. 'He must have come in that way and then locked Jonty out. Do you want to see if anything is missing? You might want to make a police report.'

Abi was certain that nothing would be missing and if there was she doubted it would matter to her, but some of the items in the apartment belonged to George and Irma. She'd have to let them know. 'I'll do it tomorrow when I've spoken to George and Irma,' she said as she folded her arms in a vain attempt to stop her body from shaking.

'Are you cold?'

Her apartment was warm and she had closed the drapes over the balcony doors to keep the draught out. She shook her head. She wasn't cold, just shaken up and probably in shock.

'Do you have any whisky?' Damien asked, as he

opened cupboards and searched the contents. He couldn't seem to stand still. Was he on edge too?

'No.'

When the search of her kitchen cupboards proved fruitless he wandered back over to the balcony doors. He opened the drapes and inspected the damage. 'Would George have anything I could use to board up these windows to make them secure overnight?'

'I'm sure he would. He has a whole shed full of carpentry stuff.'

'Would he mind if I took a look? Should I wake him up?'

'He and Irma have gone away for the weekend but I have the key to his shed.' Abi opened a kitchen drawer and pulled out a bunch of keys and handed it to Damien. Her fingers brushed his and the keys jangled as her hand shook.

'Are you going to be okay in here while I check the shed?'

'I'm fine.' She was far from okay but she was coping. Her heart rate had been settling now that she knew the house was clear but the briefest of touches from Damien made it skyrocket again. Two different triggers, one pleasant, one definitely not, but both had the power to set her heart racing. She doubted she'd be able to sleep tonight so a glass of whisky sounded like a good idea, but she'd worry about that later.

Damien disappeared again but within a few minutes Abi could hear him hammering downstairs and then he went to work on the balcony doors, using some bits of plywood he'd found in George's shed to fashion a makeshift repair job.

'I've managed to weatherproof your apartment but

it's not terribly secure. I was going to suggest that you stay over at George and Irma's but if they are away I think you should come home with me. I don't think you should stay here alone.'

'I'm not alone, I have Jonty. I can't leave him.'

'Bring him too. You can have Summer's bed and I'll put Summer in with me.'

Abi hesitated before answering and Damien mistook her hesitation for apprehension.

'Do you want to call someone and let them know you're staying with me?' he offered, realising she may have reservations about going home with him but she had no one to call. She was totally alone.

'Freya can vouch for my character,' he added. Abi had no doubt Freya would approve but if she did accept Damien's offer she wasn't sure that she wanted anyone else to know. Besides, it wasn't the fact that she was considering going home with a virtual stranger that was making her hesitate, she actually felt safe with Damien, but the fact that she was even considering the idea at all was what worried her. The fact that she *should* have reservations when she didn't was the concern. She barely knew Damien. Was it wrong to trust him so quickly?

'I don't want to put Summer out of her bed.'

Damien grinned at her and Abi was transfixed by the smile lines that appeared in the corners of his eyes. It was the only time his perfect features looked real. 'It's my bed or Summer's,' he said, 'they're the only options.'

Abi swallowed. She hadn't meant to imply anything untoward but Damien settled her nerves.

'Don't worry about Summer. She ends up in my bed most nights anyway and I'm really not going to leave you here on your own in an unsecured house. Grab what you need and come with me.'

Abi didn't need further convincing. The idea of staying in the apartment by herself made her jittery. She knew she wouldn't sleep and the idea of having company, of knowing there was someone just a room away, was far more reassuring. She had thought the apartment was secure and safe but after tonight's events she wasn't so certain. Perhaps if she still had a weapon she might have felt more comfortable but she'd returned her army-issued handgun when she'd gone on leave and she hadn't wanted to replace it. She hadn't wanted a weapon. She'd seen the damage they could do, and even now she knew she wouldn't want that responsibility or that temptation. She would rather stay at Damien's than pick up a gun.

She collected Jonty's essentials—his water bowl, lead and the large cushion that he slept on at the foot of her bed—and carried them downstairs to where Damien was loading her dog into his car. She remembered refusing Damien's invitation of a lift earlier in the week. She'd been worried then about Jonty messing up the pristine interior but she had no such qualms tonight, and neither, it seemed, did Jonty, who was more than happy to leap into the car.

Damien felt as if he'd only just drifted off to sleep when he was woken by the sound of a dog whining. He sat up in bed, disoriented, until he realised it was Jonty. What was wrong now?

He got out of bed, careful not to disturb Summer, and as he stepped into the hallway he saw the light come on in Summer's room. It shone under the door. Abi must be awake. But that didn't explain why Jonty was whining.

He should check to make sure everything was okay, but as he stretched out his hand to knock on the door the noise stopped. Should he still intrude? He had no idea. He didn't want to disturb Abi or frighten her or make a nuisance of himself, but what sort of host would he be if she needed something and he didn't offer assistance.

'Abi?' He knocked lightly and spoke through the door. 'Is everything okay?'

He opened the door and the scent of peaches wrapped around him. Abi's scent.

She was still asleep. Jonty was standing beside the bed, pushing his nose against her cheek. Did he want to go out?

But if Abi was still asleep who had turned the light on? He frowned. He was certain he had seen the light go on.

He was still standing in the doorway, trying to decide what to do, when Abi opened her eyes. He saw her jump when she registered his presence and he realised how it must look to her—an unfamiliar man appearing in her room in the middle of the night. He could see she was frightened. Her amber eyes were wide and unblinking. She reminded him of a deer caught in a spotlight and he felt like the hunter.

'Sorry, I didn't mean to frighten you.'

'Damien?'

Her cheeks were wet with tears and she was breathing heavily as if she'd been running but he knew that was impossible. There was a sheen of sweat on her brow and her hair was damp. This wasn't about Jonty needing to go outside.

'I heard Jonty whining. What's the matter?'

She sat up in bed. She was wearing one of his T-shirts

and it slipped off her shoulder to reveal a pale, creamy expanse of soft, smooth skin. They hadn't thought to grab any clothes for her, she'd been busy getting Jonty's stuff together and he hadn't given it a thought, so he'd lent her one of his T-shirts. It suited her, even though it swamped her tiny frame. With her messy hair and startled eyes she looked about twenty, although he knew she was ten years older than that. She pulled the damp T-shirt away from her body but it fell back as she let it go, clinging to her skin and drawing his attention to her nipples, which jutted against the fabric.

She was trembling.

Damien didn't hesitate any longer. In two strides he was next to the bed. In the next second he was sitting beside her. In one more second she was wrapped in his arms.

He hugged her tightly to him as he tried to stop her shaking. He had gone to her without thinking. A reflex action triggered by her fragile appearance had made him react impulsively. It seemed perfectly natural to take her in his arms and she didn't resist, didn't protest.

It *felt* perfectly natural. She was small and slight and fitted into the crook of his elbow and the curve of his shoulder as if they were designed just for her. Her head rested on his bare chest and he could feel her tears damp against his skin.

'What's wrong?'

'I had a nightmare. Jonty is trained to wake me.'

'Really? He can do that?' He made sure to keep his eyes focused on her face. The T-shirt he'd lent her was old and he hadn't realised it was quite so thin.

Abi nodded. 'He's an assistance dog. It's one of his many talents.'

'And the light? I swear I saw the light turn on when I was in the hall.'

He wasn't sure how to explain that but Abi seemed to know what he was talking about. She looked up at him. 'Jonty can flick switches.'

'You're kidding me.'

'No.'

'Is he going to make breakfast for us in the morning too?'

She smiled at him and he felt absurdly pleased that he'd managed to elicit a smile from her. 'Only for me. He's *my* assistance dog.'

'So this project you said you were involved with? You're not just training him or taking care of him? It's more personal than that?'

'Yes.'

'He's been assigned to you?'

Abi nodded.

'For nightmares?' He was trying to make sense of what was happening.

She nodded again.

'Do you have lots?' he asked.

'Only since Afghanistan.'

'Is there anything I can do?'

'Now or in general?'

'Now, for starters. Can I make you a hot chocolate? It's what I would do for Summer.'

She'd stopped shaking but she still felt cold.

'That sounds lovely but I don't need it. I'd rather you stayed here.'

He didn't need to be asked twice. It felt good to have her in his arms and he wasn't going to pretend otherwise.

He leant back against the bedhead and swung his

legs up on top of the quilt, stretching them out in front of him. Abi stayed curled against his chest and he kept his arm around her shoulders as he felt the steady, rhythmical rise and fall of her breathing. She seemed calmer now but he wasn't surprised to hear that she had nightmares. He could only imagine what she would have seen in Afghanistan. What she would have been through. What he didn't know was whether it would help to talk about her dreams or if it was best to ignore the horrors of the past in the hope that she could put it behind her. Would talking about it make it better or worse?

He couldn't remember much from his psychology studies. What would be the recommended practice today?

He decided to try talking about it. If she didn't want to talk to him she'd soon tell him. She didn't seem to have a problem with telling him if she thought he had overstepped the mark or was wrong. She'd put him back in his place a couple of times already this week.

'Is it always the same dream?' he asked.

'Pretty much.'

Silence fell and he thought that was it. If she didn't want to talk about it he wasn't going to force the issue.

She shifted her position, turning her head so she was looking at the ceiling. Had that been a protective movement designed so that he couldn't see her face? So he couldn't feel the dampness of her tears?

She started talking. 'In the dream I'm in Kabul. It's always Kabul, even if sometimes it doesn't look like it. Sometimes it looks like LA or Phoenix but I still know I'm in Kabul. It's hot and dusty, crowded and chaotic. There are people shouting and jostling. Traffic noise, car horns, brakes, engines revving, sirens.

Big-city noises and big-city smells—diesel fumes and
garbage. I always have the impression of Kabul as loud
and kind of manic but then the mania goes up a notch.
One minute it's just regular bedlam, and then an explosion rips through the crowd, showering everyone
with debris, intensifying the chaos. I can feel the force
of the blast. It knocks me off my feet and for a moment
everything is silent. In my dream I know instantly that
a bomb has exploded but it wasn't like that at the time.'

At the time? This dream was real? Or rather the
events in the dream were real? No wonder she had
woken up in a cold sweat.

'The beginning of the dream is always the same,' she
continued, 'but the actual explosion takes me by surprise every time. After the bomb explodes the dream
varies. I can never change the beginning, the bomb always goes off, but what happens next changes, although
it's always bad, just different degrees of terrible, and I
can't control it.'

'What happens next?' he asked, not sure he was prepared for the answer, but if she needed to talk he would
listen.

'My commanding officer is there too. He's injured
and I try to help him. In my dream I crawl across the
ground. I can feel glass and stones and metal cutting
into my hands and knees but all I can see is Mark lying
on the ground. He's not moving and I don't know if he's
breathing. I keep crawling but this bit varies. Sometimes I reach him and sometimes I feel like I'm just
crawling for minute after minute, never getting any
closer. Sometimes Mark dies before I can reach him
and sometimes I get there while he's still alive. He has
a wife and daughters, sometimes they are in my dream

too, but they do nothing, just stand and watch and ask me why I'm not saving him. Why aren't I doing more? I don't have anything to tell them except that I am trying, but the end is always the same. Mark dies and I wake up crying.'

'You were actually caught up in a situation like that? This was real?'

She nodded. 'We had gone into Kabul for a meeting, me, my commanding officer, Mark, and another captain. We were leaving the meeting to head back to the base. It was around lunchtime, the streets were busy as they always were, crowded with cars, trucks, motorbikes and pedestrians. Our driver was waiting on the street to collect us. He was out of the truck, holding the back door open for Mark, when there was an explosion. There was no warning, although I don't know why I would have expected one. One minute I was rounding the back of the truck and the next I was knocked off my feet.'

'Were you hurt?'

She shook her head and her hair brushed across his chest. 'Not critically. When a bomb explodes there're degrees of injury—dead, critically injured, non-life-threatening injuries and okay. Some of the blood was mine but I wasn't badly injured. My ears were ringing but other than that I could hear nothing else for what seemed like minutes but was probably only seconds. The air was thick with dust and smoke. I was disorientated but I had worked out what had happened. A bomb had been detonated, but I didn't know what sort or where. Not that it mattered. It had succeeded in creating the damage it had been designed for. I can remember lying there, fighting to breathe but being unable to move because I had no air. When I did catch my breath my throat and tongue were coated with dust. I inhaled and I could smell burnt flesh and the metallic tang of blood but I didn't realise some of it was mine.

'When I got up my leg gave way beneath me. I had shrapnel embedded in my thigh but I hadn't realised it. My leg wouldn't support my weight, which was probably lucky. It was a stupid idea to try to stand up. It would be safer to stay low but I wasn't thinking clearly.'

Damien could scarcely believe what he was hearing. He'd seen images from Afghanistan but he'd never really spent much time thinking about the people who were caught up in the war. It had all seemed to be so remote. Until now. Until he was listening to Abi's recount and feeling her tremble in his arms and seeing the fear and confusion in her eyes.

'I could see the other captain lying on the ground ahead of me. He had already walked around to the far side of the vehicle, which had sheltered him from the force of the blast. He was groggy and probably concussed but otherwise uninjured. I thought we'd been lucky. I thought we'd escaped any real damage but it turned out that wasn't the case. I dragged myself around to the other side of the truck, looking for the others— my CO and the driver. People were screaming now and crying. Running. Falling. It was complete chaos, there was no sense of order, just panic.

'We needed to get out of there but when I got around the vehicle I found that our driver was dead. And he wasn't the only one. There were plenty of dead and injured. My commanding officer had been hit. He was bleeding from his side, frothing blood from his lips. He must have thrown his arms up when the bomb exploded. It would have been a reflex reaction but it meant that he'd exposed the area under his arm, a gap in his flak jacket, and shrapnel had ripped through his chest wall. He'd sustained serious chest wounds and I knew I was unlikely to be able to save him but I had to try. There were others I could have tried to help but I didn't. Mark was my priority, my responsibility.

'I was kneeling in the middle of the road, trying to plug the wound in his chest with my hands. It was hopeless. There was a first-aid kit in the truck, a good one, a combat one, but I needed a hospital. There was nothing I could do in that environment. It wasn't safe. We had to get out of there. We had no idea what would happen next.

'The other captain helped me to lift Mark into the truck and then we had to load the body of our driver as well, we couldn't leave him. Everything had happened so quickly there was no time really to think, only to react. We had to get away but I still think about all those injured Afghans we left behind, even though I know my duty of care was to my own team. That was my priority.

'All the way back to the base I fought to keep Mark alive. The first-aid kit was substantial. I had bags of saline and bandages but what I needed was units of blood and an operating theatre. I knew he was unlikely to make it but I had to try. He was dead before we reached the base.'

'It sounds like you did everything you could. Even if there had been a whole team working on him, it sounds like the outcome would have been the same.'

'I know that, but it was the first time I couldn't save someone I knew well, and that's a hard thing to let go of. I think that's why I keep replaying the day in my dreams, hoping that it ends differently, but it never does.

It always ends the same way. With people dying. I feel guilty that I couldn't save him, I feel guilty sometimes that I survived when so many others didn't. I've never met Mark's wife and daughters but they turn up in my dream as my guilty subconscious.'

'Have you spoken to someone about this?'

'Officially?'

Damien nodded.

'I have. I've been diagnosed with PTSD and the military medical corps insist on therapy for all personnel even while on leave.'

'You're on leave? I thought you'd left?'

'I can't apply for a discharge from the army, it has to be recommended.'

'Do you think you should be working? Shouldn't you be taking some time to recover?'

'I need to stay busy. Work gives me something else to focus on. Without that I have nothing and I can't sit around with just my thoughts for company. I've been assessed as being fit to work but not fit for active duty. I can't work in a combat support unit but a hospital that's not in a war zone is fine. And I feel safe at work.'

'You don't feel safe generally?'

'I get nervous in unfamiliar, noisy or crowded environments so I try to avoid them if possible, but sometimes I can't, which is why Jonty was assigned to me, to help prevent panic attacks.'

'Should I have brought Summer to stay at your house? Has being in a strange place triggered your nightmare?' Damien felt terrible, as if this was somehow his fault.

'Maybe,' she said, making him feel even worse. 'But

I think it was more likely to be an after-effect of the shock of the break-in.'

The break-in had threatened her safety, Damien realised, and that thought eased his conscience slightly, although not completely. He needed to fix this.

'What can I do? How can I help?'

'Would you stay with me? Just until I fall asleep? I'm scared I'll have another dream.' Her voice was quiet and it sounded almost as if she expected him to refuse.

How could he refuse? He didn't want to. 'Sure.'

He half lay in the bed, with his shoulders propped against the headboard and Abi's head resting on his chest. Summer's bed was narrow and Abi had to lie on her side to fit. She curled herself against him and he wrapped his arm around her shoulders to keep her in the bed. He doubted whether either of them were going to go back to sleep and he wasn't planning on leaving her here alone if she did succumb.

He reached across and switched off the bedside light. He could feel Abi's eyelashes fluttering against his bare skin and each tiny puff of air as she exhaled. He usually slept naked but because he'd had to share his bed with Summer he'd put a pair of boxer shorts on so at least he was semi-decent. Although he didn't think thin boxer shorts were going to be enough of a shield against the touch of Abi's fingers and the smell of her hair.

Her fingers rested lightly on his chest and her head was tucked under his chin. He definitely wasn't going to be able to go back to sleep now.

The hall light was still on, taking the edge off the darkness, and he lay in the shadows and stared at the ceiling and thought about the enigma that was Abi.

She intrigued him. She'd been in his life for less

than a week but something told him she was going to leave a lasting effect. There was something fascinating about her. She was fragile and damaged but he sensed an underlying strength of character that suggested she would not be easily defeated. Where had that strength come from?

Her breathing slowed and she drifted off and he could feel his resistance weaken as she slept in his arms. He had vowed not to get involved with a woman again, he didn't have the time or the energy, but Abi was making him revise his thinking.

She was an anomaly, a mixture of courage and strength, fragility and insecurity, and she stirred a mixture of emotions in him. He wanted to know more about her. He'd never met anyone quite like her and he wanted to make the time to find out what made her tick.

In recent times his world had revolved around his daughter and his work. He didn't socialise and even when he had it had been with Brooke and her actor friends. He had never really understood them, never been sure what was real and what was fake, but Abi felt real. He was drawn to her. She was interesting and gorgeous, smart and strong, and yet he sensed some self-doubt in her. Had she always had that or was it the lasting effect of her CO's death?

He had noticed her hesitation when they had walked into the party last night. He hadn't expected that. Brooke had always been self-confident, she would have walked into a party and stopped and waited until everyone had looked at her. She would have arrived late so that she could ensure there were people there to notice her arrival. She'd had the behaviour of a celebrity even before she'd become one.

Abi was so confident in a work situation that he'd expected the same generally, and her reluctance, her lack of confidence, had surprised him. Had something else happened to her? The story she'd told about the bomb didn't explain it. She'd acted quickly, selflessly and bravely, she hadn't acted like a person lacking in self-confidence. He was certain there was more to her story and he was keen to find out what it was.

He wanted to know the answers, all the answers.

He turned his head and watched her sleep until fatigue overcame him too.

When he woke in the morning he'd been dreaming of sunshine, of peaches ripening in the summer sun.

Abi was still curled against him. Her breasts were squashed against his chest and her hand rested on his stomach. He was still shirtless. He should have gone back to his bed once she'd fallen asleep but he hadn't wanted to leave her alone. If he was completely honest he was enjoying the feeling of a woman, this woman, in his arms and he hadn't wanted to let her go. One of Abi's thighs was tucked between his, slight and warm. His hand had moved south from her shoulders and was resting on her hip. He could feel his erection, swollen, throbbing, pleading for release. Her hair smelled like peaches and her skin was the colour of vanilla ice cream. She was soft and sweet and delicious. It had been a while since he'd had anyone quite as delightful in his bed and he wasn't averse to the idea of exploring her attractions.

The quilt had slipped off her leg and from beneath the hem of her T-shirt, *his* T-shirt, he could see the shrapnel scars on her thigh. He replayed the story she'd told him in the night and remembered she was tougher than she looked. He ran his fingers lightly over the scars. They were raised and darker than her skin, reminiscent of a raspberry swirl in vanilla ice cream. A legacy of her past and a reminder that she was a survivor.

Abi stirred at his touch. Her eyelashes fluttered and her amber eyes opened. He could see her taking a moment to work out where she was.

He didn't want her to panic. She brought out all his protective instincts, which were never far from the surface anyway. He knew he had a habit of wanting to look after women, to protect them, a desire that stemmed from his upbringing. His mother suffered from debilitating rheumatoid arthritis and his father had been her primary source of care and support and that sense of protectiveness was strongly instilled in him. There was something vulnerable about Abi and he didn't want any more harm to come to her, not if it was in his power to prevent that.

'You're okay, Abi,' he told her. 'You're in Summer's bed.'

She woke properly and he could tell she was embarrassed to find herself draped across him. Not that he was complaining. She moved away from him, pulling her thigh out from between his legs and lifting her hand from his stomach, leaving a palm-sized patch of skin that felt cooler now she was gone.

Her eyes ran over his body, making his erection stand to attention even more than before. Her gaze moved from his bare chest down over his abdominals and further south. There was no way to disguise his reaction to her and he didn't want to. As far as he was concerned, there was nothing wrong with letting her see what effect she had on him.

He saw her swallow and when she looked up at him there was a question in the golden depths of her eyes.

She pulled farther away and he resisted the urge to hold her close. He didn't want to let her go but he didn't want to frighten her either. He relaxed his arm around her shoulders, giving her space.

'We didn't, did we?'

He shook his head. 'No. That would always be your decision.' His words were more of a question than a statement. It was obvious to both of them that he was keen but he would never make a presumption about sex. Both parties had to be willing and he was curious to know her thoughts but she gave a tiny shake of her head.

'I can't.'

That was more hopeful than a 'no' and better than an 'I don't want to' but it wasn't a 'yes'.

'Can't or won't?' he asked.

'Can't,' she clarified. 'We can't. Summer is in the house. This is her room. What if she comes in?'

She had a point but her answer gave him hope. He suspected she might be just as willing as he was in different circumstances but he wasn't going to push her, he wasn't going to take advantage. He would bide his time, certain that it would come in the not-too-distant future.

He wasn't sure exactly when he'd changed his mind, when he'd begun to feel like he wanted to pursue her, when he'd begun to think that women *weren't* too much trouble, well, one woman in particular. Had it been last night, when she'd curled into his side, or the night of the party when he'd given her a lift and his car had been filled with the scent of fresh peaches, or the afternoon that she had collected Summer from school and he'd so badly wanted to kiss her?

He knew this attraction was fraught with danger. He knew there were all sorts of reasons why he should keep his distance—they were colleagues, she had issues, he had baggage, he was a single dad with a difficult ex-wife and his priorities should be on Summer—but it was hard to ignore the stirring of desire when he'd held her in his arms. It had felt good. It had reminded him that he was a man.

The throbbing in his groin was another strong indicator that all his manly bits were working but he'd have to relieve the tension himself. He would do well to remember to focus on other aspects and keep a lid on his attraction to Abi. He wasn't planning on ignoring it altogether but he needed to slow things down. He couldn't jump in, he didn't know how she felt and he wasn't sure if he was ready. There were lots of complicating factors. It would be a different story perhaps if they'd met in a bar or at a conference, if she didn't already know Summer, if they didn't work together, if she hadn't spent the night in his arms.

'Just so I know, in case we ever find ourselves in this position again, how would Jonty react? Is he trained to attack?' His question lightened the mood, as he'd hoped it would. It let Abi back out of this situation but also made his intentions clear. He would slow things down but he wouldn't give up completely.

'Does he look like he's about to attack?' she countered, and Damien glanced over to where the dog lay, fast asleep, on his cushion, completely oblivious to what was going on around him.

'People who need assistance dogs often need them

for things like panic attacks, PTSD or epilepsy,' she explained. 'They might need help from paramedics or the public so it wouldn't be useful if the dogs were trained to protect their owners and not let people close.'

'Good to know.' He smiled and stood up, disentangling himself from Abi. 'But I guess it's time for me to shower and take care of some business.' His erection was plainly obvious in his boxer shorts and he still made no attempt to hide it. He left her lying in the bed and hoped he was giving her plenty to think about.

Abi stretched lazily as she watched Damien walk out of the room. She'd slept soundly and had woken up feeling relaxed and comfortable for the first time in months. It was amazing the difference having a warm, hard body in the bed with her had made. She had felt safe, and feeling safe had allowed her to sleep peacefully. She hadn't had a recurrence of the nightmare, she hadn't dreamt of Mark, but perhaps that wasn't surprising given that a half-naked Damien had lain beside her.

He moved gracefully on his long legs and she wondered if he was a good dancer. He looked fluid and she could imagine him on the dance floor, could imagine herself in his arms. She felt a blush steal across her cheeks. Thank God he had his back to her and couldn't see her devouring him with her eyes. His black boxer shorts left very little to her imagination. His body was lean and muscular, and she knew exactly how it had felt under her fingers, warm and firm. Her hand had been spread across his stomach, her fingers resting on the ridges of his abdominals. She was mortified to think that she'd been draped across him when she'd woken up but relieved to know that nothing more sexual had happened. It was clear that he wouldn't have minded. Should she be flattered by that or nervous?

She felt both flattered and nervous but she was also hesitant.

She had ignored his obvious erection, or had tried to, but her hesitation had had nothing to do with the fact that his young daughter was in the house. Summer had been a factor but not the ultimate deciding factor. Abi had made a promise to herself. No more colleagues. No more men with baggage.

Summer's presence was a reason but she hadn't been the problem. The problem was Abi herself.

She was damaged.

She was still recovering.

But most of all she was afraid.

CHAPTER SIX

ABI WAS AFRAID of lots of things. Of getting hurt. Of getting involved. Of jumping in before she'd tested the water. But she couldn't tell Damien that.

Ironic, considering all the things she'd told him last night, but in the reality of the morning she was embarrassed about confiding in him. She wished she hadn't said anything but she couldn't take it back now.

Her psychologist had been encouraging her to talk to others about her experiences and feelings but Abi had no one to confide in. She had no one to spend time with, no family and no friends, she had lost touch with any friends who were not in the army and in the wake of Mark's death she certainly didn't want to spend time with army acquaintances. Which left her with no one.

She had to admit that it had been a relief of sorts to talk to Damien about her experience but she wasn't quite sure what had prompted her to do so. Had he caught her at a moment of weakness when she hadn't been thinking straight, or had she downloaded because she felt safe?

She'd been thrown by the break-in and then by being in a strange bed. Her nightmare had unsettled her further, as had waking up in Damien's arms. At first she'd thought she was dreaming but that dream had been much nicer than her recurring nightmare.

Abi wondered what it meant that she had been prepared to tell him about her experience, about the circumstances of Mark's death, but that she still hadn't told him everything. She hadn't told him she and Mark had been lovers and she knew it was because she didn't want him to think badly of her. Neither did she want him to see her as someone who had affairs with married men, even though she hadn't known that Mark had been married until he'd died. She'd known he'd had two daughters but he'd told her he was divorced. It had only been at his funeral that she'd discovered he'd lied to her. But would Damien think that was a suitable defence? She hadn't known Mark was married but she still felt guilty and she wasn't prepared to expose herself to Damien in case he judged her. Why did his opinion matter so much? Why had she confided in him?

Could she behave as if nothing had happened?

She'd have to, she thought as he came back into the room.

He had showered and was dressed in jeans and a T-shirt, and he held a cup of coffee in one hand and a pile of clothes in the other.

He passed her the coffee and put the clothes on the end of the bed. 'You didn't bring any clothes with you and I wasn't sure if you wanted to eat breakfast in your evening gown. You might be more comfortable in something from this pile.'

'Thank you,' she said, as she surveyed the pile. He'd brought a pair of his track pants with a drawstring waist, an old university sweater and a white towelling dressing gown. Everything would be miles too big for her, except maybe the dressing gown. She wondered who it belonged to but wasn't about to ask.

The bedroom door opened and Summer wandered in, rubbing the sleep from her eyes. 'Good morning, sunshine,' Damien greeted her, but she wasn't interested in her father. She only had eyes for Abi.

'Abi? Why are you in my bed?'

Abi hadn't given any thought to what they would tell Summer but fortunately Damien had an answer ready.

'Abi's house was damaged.'

'How?'

'A raccoon got inside and broke a window.'

Abi choked back a laugh. She was pleased Damien hadn't told Summer the real story—that wasn't something a five-year-old needed to hear—but she hadn't expected him to be quite so elaborate with his storytelling. 'I was worried about the rain getting in so Abi stayed here.'

Summer happily accepted Damien's embellishment of the truth. Abi guessed at her age she still believed in fairytales and Damien's tale was almost believable.

'Okay, let's give Abi some privacy. You can come and help me make the pancakes.' He turned to Abi. 'That's our Sunday morning tradition. Why don't you get dressed and join us?'

Abi showered and wrapped the dressing gown around herself. She had debated wearing Damien's clothes, but despite the fact that she'd worn his T-shirt last night—she'd been too distressed to think clearly then—now that she'd calmed down she decided it would have felt odd to step into Damien's clothes. It would feel far too intimate.

More intimate than sharing a bed? she questioned herself. Under the circumstances, she decided it would.

She could smell pancakes. She belted the gown tightly at the waist and followed her nose. Summer was feeding Jonty a pancake when she wandered into the kitchen. She checked Jonty's paw, relieved to find that he didn't appear to be suffering any after-effects from the glass fragment getting stuck in his foot, nothing that a pancake breakfast wouldn't fix anyway.

Damien had another coffee waiting for her on the kitchen bench, plus juice, maple syrup for the pancakes and a bowl of oranges. He had a tea towel tucked into the back pocket of his jeans and he looked at home in the kitchen. Abi was a terrible cook. She didn't have a big appetite and there was no point cooking for one, and in the army she'd always had meals prepared for her so there had been no need to learn. She could get used to having Damien cook for her but she kept that thought to herself.

She was on her second pancake—they were delicious, light and fluffy—and for some reason this morning her appetite was flourishing, when Damien spoke to Summer.

'Okay, sunshine, what would you like to do today?' Summer had finished her breakfast and had a computer tablet booted up on the kitchen bench. 'Have you checked the weather?' Damien asked as she swiped her finger across the screen. 'Is there any rain?'

'Nope.'

'Outdoors, then.'

'Can Abi choose?'

'Choose what?' Abi asked.

'Sunday is our day to explore LA,' Damien told her. 'Summer usually chooses the activity and I'll work out where we can go.'

'You could choose somewhere, Abi, and then you could come with us,' Summer added.

'I'm not really dressed for a day out. I need to go home and make arrangements to fix the "raccoon" damage.' She made her excuses, sure Damien didn't need or want her tagging along with them. This sounded like father-daughter time that she didn't need to intrude into.

'You could borrow my mum's clothes.' Summer's statement was very matter-of-fact, as if she saw nothing unusual in other women helping themselves to her mother's wardrobe.

'Your mum's clothes?'

Summer was nodding. 'She has heaps of clothes.'

'Summer, why don't you take Jonty out into the garden for a minute?' Damien suggested. Had he noticed Abi's expression?

She waited until Summer left the room before asking the question. 'I was under the impression that you and Summer's mother weren't together?'

'We're not.'

'But her things are here?'

'Some of her things.'

Did that mean she was still here or did she come and go as she pleased? What if she arrived now and found Abi sitting at her kitchen bench? Abi had assumed from Damien's comments that he was single but had she chosen to believe that? Wanted to believe that? Had he encouraged her to think that?

'Whose robe am I wearing?'

'Not hers.'

She didn't want to ask the next question. If it wasn't Brooke's, who did it belong too? She didn't want to know. She had already been told more than she wanted to hear.

'Does she still have a key?'

'Yes.'

'How could you bring me here if she still has access? What if she walks in?' Even though nothing had happened between them Abi felt completely stupid. She should have stuck to her guns, not just fallen in with Damien's wishes. Why hadn't she resisted him? What had happened to the Abi who'd used to be so independent minded and strong? Since Afghanistan it seemed as if her reason and logic had deserted her. Had Mark's lies and deceit shaken her confidence so much that now she didn't trust herself to make good choices? Was she so eager for company, so lonely that she would forsake her principles and blindly follow where someone else led?

She needed to consider her motives. Why had she agreed to come home with him? Was it because she hadn't felt safe to stay home alone or was it because she found him attractive? Had she been thinking with her hormones or her head? She couldn't afford to think with her hormones. Danger lay down that path. It had got her into trouble before. She needed to be calm, methodical, rational. She needed to make measured decisions and sound judgements. She couldn't jump into something without consideration of her own motives or his. She didn't want to get into the middle of something.

'Abi, Brooke is in New York, she's not about to walk in and find you here, and this isn't her house anymore.

She doesn't live here.' His voice was calm and patient. 'She's just storing some of her stuff here. She has far too many clothes and hasn't been able to take them all with her. They're in the spare room. She's my ex-wife, we're divorced. What I do is none of her business as long as it's not hurting Summer.'

'Well, I'm still not wearing her clothes.'

'Fair enough. I didn't suggest that you should.'

He was right. It had been Summer's suggestion. She had bitten his head off for no reason. But was it for no reason? She only had his word for what the situation was. How did she know he was telling the truth? She didn't have a good track record when it came to picking trustworthy men. Once again, this could just be a case of a man telling her what he thought she wanted to hear.

She wasn't sure but did it matter?

It shouldn't matter to her what the situation was between Damien and his ex-wife. She hadn't done anything to regret yet but she wouldn't apologise, just in case. And she wouldn't spend the day with them. It would be best if she put some distance between her and them. She couldn't afford to get involved.

She took her empty plate to the sink. 'I'll call a cab,' she said. 'I need to go home.'

'I'll take you. It's only two blocks. Summer and I can wait for you to get changed and then you're welcome to spend the day with us if you'd like to.'

'No, I can't. I really do need to go home and organise to get my windows fixed.'

'I'll take care of that,' he offered. 'I'd like your company.'

Abi hesitated.

'Say yes because if you don't *you* can tell Summer

why you're not joining us,' Damien added as his daughter opened the back door to step inside.

'What are we going to do?' Summer asked.

Abi looked at Damien. She could see the challenge in his eyes, daring her to join them. But she didn't know if she could.

'You get to choose where we go,' he told her, and his voice was quiet, reassuring. 'You can choose somewhere you'll feel comfortable.'

Could she do this?

She realised with surprise that she wanted to. What was the harm in making a spontaneous decision? She used to do that all the time but since Mark's death she'd felt constrained by her fear. She had to remember that bad things didn't always happen, things didn't always go wrong. But where should they go?

Somewhere outside, she thought. Being winter, an outside venue was unlikely to be crowded, especially if they went early. 'Maybe we could walk to the Santa Monica Pier,' she suggested.

'Walk to the pier? Nobody walks in LA,' Damien teased.

Abi relaxed as Damien messed about. It felt good not to over think things for a change, not to worry about every decision. She took a deep breath; she could do this.

'The exercise will do us good,' she said, hoping that Damien didn't suggest that she walk and he'd meet her there. She really didn't want to walk to the pier on her own. She had set walks that she took Jonty on, streets she knew, past houses she was familiar with. And she didn't want to walk to the pier without Damien. He made her feel safe. She was pretty sure that Summer would choose to go with Jonty, which meant that Damien would choose to go with Summer. At least, she hoped she would.

'Can I hold Jonty's lead?' Summer asked.

'Of course.'

Abi smiled at Damien, pleased to get her own way, and he laughed. 'Why did I bother arguing against two women?'

'We'll compromise,' Abi said. 'Let's drive down past the Beach House and walk half the distance to the pier. That's only about a mile each way.'

Damien and Summer drove Abi home and while he waited for her to change he organised a glazier to do the repair work later in the day. Abi was used to managing on her own but she had to admit she liked the feeling of having someone else to look out for her. She didn't feel as if she'd been doing such a great job of taking care of herself of late.

Damien drove them to the Annenberg Beach House, where they piled out of the car to walk to the pier. Summer walked next to Abi, holding Jonty's lead with one hand and Abi's hand with the other. Her hand was tiny and warm and Abi could feel herself becoming more enthralled with Summer and the idea of motherhood. That was something she'd always had mixed feelings about because of her own childhood. She wasn't sure if she had the right genetic make-up for parenthood. Both of her parents were screw-ups and while she would love a chance to have a family of her own, one that wouldn't leave her, she had always had a fear that maybe she wouldn't cope either, just like her parents hadn't. But Summer was gorgeous and Abi could feel a tug on her heartstrings as the little girl skipped along beside her, keeping up a one-way conversation with Jonty.

Even walking at the pace of a five-year-old and with a dog who liked to stop and sniff everything in his path, they still made it to the pier just as it opened, which meant, to Abi's relief, that they had beaten the crowds.

'Where to first?' Damien asked.

'The carousel,' Summer shouted.

The carousel was indoors and as they entered the building Abi immediately scoped out all the exits. It was a habit she had formed in the past six months. She needed to know the quickest way out of a building or a potentially dangerous situation. Summer hopped up onto one of the carousel horses as Abi got her bearings then chose to sit in the sleigh, which allowed Jonty to come onto the carousel with her but it also left room for Damien.

He sat beside her as that position allowed him to keep an eye on Summer. The sleigh was narrow, the seat just big enough for two. Jonty sat at Abi's feet but Abi was aware of Damien's thigh pressing against hers, the heat radiating from his body burning through her exercise pants.

Going on the carousel had been a mistake. Not only did it put her too close to Damien but the high sides and back restricted her view. As the music began to play Abi could feel her anxiety level building. She felt hemmed in, trapped, and as the carousel started to turn, panic really set in. She was losing sight of the exits, her sense of direction was being compromised by the rotation of the carousel, and the noise and repetition of the music was making it hard to concentrate. She reached down to stroke Jonty's coat as she tried to calm herself. Her eyes darted back and forth as she tried to keep an exit in sight. Her breaths were becoming more rapid; she could hear herself panting.

'Are you okay?' Damien asked, but Abi couldn't answer. She opened her mouth but she couldn't form the words. She didn't know the answer.

'You'll be all right,' he said, putting his hand on her knee. 'You're safe.'

But Abi knew that wasn't necessarily true. Bad things could and did happen unexpectedly, despite what she'd told herself earlier.

Damien lifted his hand from her leg and covered her hand with his. 'Focus on me,' he said, but now all she could think about was the sensation of her hand in his. Perhaps that was his point. She looked down, focusing on their fingers and the way his had wrapped around hers. His hand warmed hers and distracted her.

'Look at me,' he told her, and she lifted her eyes.

She looked into his eyes. They were dark and intense and everything around her blurred and disappeared until all that was left was Damien. The building and the ride merged into blank surroundings, indistinguishable from each other. Even the carousel music seemed muted. Only Damien was in sharp relief.

'I'll keep you safe. Trust me,' he said. 'Do you trust me?'

She wanted to trust him but she'd been let down too many times in the past. 'I have trouble with trust.'

'The ride is nearly over.' His voice was quiet and sure. 'You're okay. You're safe.'

The ride slowed and the music ceased and the building came back into focus. Abi looked around. She was safe, she could see no immediate threats, but she needed to get outside; needed to escape these four walls. She stood up, eager to get off the carousel. Her legs were shaky but Damien kept hold of her hand, steadying her.

Summer was already down off her horse. 'Can I have another turn?' she asked, but Abi barely heard her.

'Not right now.'

Abi was itching to make a run for it but Damien hadn't let go of her hand. She tried taking some deep breaths, focusing on the connection with Damien. Letting his strength anchor her, allowing him to stop her from taking flight. She had Jonty's lead in one hand, Damien in the other. She should be okay.

'But I want to ride on the bunny rabbit,' Summer insisted.

'Jonty needs some fresh air,' Damien told her, and that was the end of the discussion. Summer didn't bother to argue further. At the moment, whatever Jonty needed he got. He was Summer's number-one priority. Abi forced her legs to move towards the exit as she wondered if she should suggest that Damien get Summer a dog of her own. It would be good company for her if she was destined to be an only child. Abi knew how much Jonty's company had come to mean to her and she could imagine how much she would have loved a dog growing up. She saw a lot of similarities between her own childhood and Summer's situation, though with one big difference. Summer had a father who adored her but that didn't necessarily mean he had the time to devote to her. A dog would be a distraction, a responsibility and a companion for her.

Summer skipped ahead of them and if she noticed Damien and Abi holding hands she didn't comment. Abi pulled her hand from Damien's as they followed

Summer outside. As nice as it felt, it also made her feel uncomfortable.

Summer was heading towards the Beach Bounce, a trampoline and bungee harness contraption that allowed children, or adults, to jump and twist and turn without the danger of falling. 'What about this?' she asked. 'Can I try it?'

Damien turned to Abi. 'Will you be okay here?' he asked.

Abi needed to be where she could keep an eye on the situation, where she would be able to see what was coming her way. The Beach Bounce was on the edge of the pier. She could stand on the far side of the trampoline so that her back was to the water as she faced the pier. No one could come up behind her. She nodded and made her way around the trampoline.

Damien paid for Summer's ticket, put her into the queue and then came to stand with Abi.

'Shouldn't you wait with Summer?' Abi asked. Her anxiety was still in hyper-drive.

'I can watch her from here. It will be her turn in a few minutes.'

Abi kept her back to the water and let her eyes roam over the pier. Jonty sat on her right and Damien stood to her left. He was turned slightly sideways, shielding her a little, his posture protective, and she felt quite safe.

'She hasn't been on this before?' Abi asked as she watched Summer, who had been strapped into the harness and was now turning somersaults and bouncing higher and higher as her confidence built.

'No. I don't remember this being here last time we came to the pier or perhaps she was too small. Lots of the rides have a height restriction.'

'Why are you spending your Sundays out exploring LA?' she asked.

'I'm from San Francisco originally but we moved here two years ago. Brooke pushed for the move to further her career. I admit I resisted the idea but when it became clear that she would go with or without me I realised I had to move, for Summer's sake.'

So he had moved for his family, for Brooke, and now she had taken off again, this time to New York. Abi wondered whether he would follow Brooke again, for Summer's sake. She would do well to remember that he was a man who came with baggage.

'Do you miss San Francisco?'

Damien nodded. 'I do. It's taken me a while to feel like I belong here, I'm still not sure that I do. I love working at The Hills but LA is a completely different type of city and we're still finding our feet. What about you? Where did you grow up?'

'Here.'

'Here? You're a native?'

'We do exist, you know.'

'I know, it's just that almost everyone I've met has moved here from somewhere else.'

'That's the movie business, no doubt.'

'I guess so. So you'd be the perfect tour guide for me and Summer, then. You could show us all your favourite childhood haunts.'

'I think my childhood might have been different from the one you're imagining. It would certainly be different from the one you'd be dreaming of for Summer.'

'What do you mean by that?'

Abi wasn't sure how to answer. She found it odd that

Damien wanted to know about her. She wasn't used to talking about herself—in fact, she usually tried to avoid it unless it was in a controlled environment, like with her therapist.

'I didn't have the idyllic childhood you might be picturing. I never knew my father, he abandoned us shortly after I was born, and my mother...' Abi paused. Even after thirty years she always hesitated when it came to describing her mother. She'd loved Abi in the best way she'd known how but she'd suffered from depression, which had manifested into substance abuse, mostly alcohol, and there had been plenty of times when Abi had just had to manage as best she could. Despite Summer's mother's failing in the child-raising department, she doubted it would match those of her own mother. 'Let's say she struggled to cope with raising me on her own. We didn't spend weekends at the pier or at theme parks.' Abi had spent a lot of her childhood alone.

'Is your mum still in LA?'

Abi shook her head. 'She's dead.'

'I'm sorry. Was it recent?'

'No. She died in a car accident just after I turned eighteen.' Abi had been alone for almost half her life. Long enough to be used to it, and to know she didn't like it, but not long enough to get over the guilt.

She had left home at seventeen to join the army. She'd been unable to continue to live with her mother, she couldn't be responsible for her any more, but she had always blamed herself a bit for the accident. She wondered if it would have made a difference if she hadn't left but she'd known she'd had to get away. Her home life had been toxic. She had never known whether her mother had suffered from depression before her father had left them. She could have had post-natal depression which had perhaps been exacerbated by Abi's father's abandonment, but, whatever the cause or the reason, her mother had turned to alcohol as her crutch and one day she had crashed her car into a tree. Abi had wondered if it had been suicide but had never been sure. She'd just been so relieved that no one else had been hurt.

She still carried the guilt. For her mother's death, among other things. Her therapist had told her time and again that she was not responsible for her mother's accident or her father's abandonment or Mark's death, but Abi found it difficult to move on. She had carried so much guilt for so long that she didn't know how to let it go.

Caroline had also told her she needed to talk about these things, that it didn't help to bottle things up and let them fester. She had suggested that if she talked about them she took away the power they had to hurt her, that it would make the problems smaller, but Abi didn't know how to do that.

Summer's turn on the Beach Bounce finished and Abi was happy to let her take over the conversation and distract her from her thoughts by leading them around the pier. They followed her past numerous rides and sideshows before she stopped at the basketball hoops and insisted that Damien have a turn.

He shrugged out of his jacket and asked Abi to hold it for him. He slung it around her shoulders when she agreed. It was warm and comforting, a bit like being wrapped in his arms again. It felt safe.

Removing his jacket had left him standing before her in his shirtsleeves. His arms were muscular and he could pick up the basketball in one hand with his long fingers. She watched as he transferred the ball from his left hand to his right before throwing it. He was quick and accurate and it wasn't until the game was finished that Abi realised she had forgotten to be nervous, she'd been too busy admiring Damien's skill and physique.

He had scored enough points to win a soft toy for Summer and she chose a seahorse covered in pink and silver sequins layered like scales. Abi wasn't certain that seahorses actually had scales but she supposed it didn't matter—a soft toy didn't need to be a perfect replica of the real thing. Come to think of it, seahorses probably weren't pink and silver either. But not everything in the world had to be perfect. Sometimes it was okay to have some imagination and succumb to fantasies. Summer was reminding Abi of what it was like to be a child, to believe that good things could happen, how to have fun.

'You have to have another turn, Daddy,'

'I think one toy is enough, Summer, especially as I know I'll end up carrying it *and* you.'

'It's not for me. Abi needs a toy too.'

Damien looked at Abi. 'In that case…' he said, and Abi felt warmth flow through her. To think he was doing this for her.

Summer wriggled her way between Abi and Jonty as Damien tossed balls through the hoop. Summer was rubbing Jonty's head with one hand but Abi felt her other hand slide into her own as they watched. It was tiny and warm and the contact melted Abi's heart.

'What takes your fancy, ma'am?' he asked as he turned around at the end of the game, victorious once more. He was smiling broadly and Abi sensed he was enjoying the day as much as she was. She was pretty sure she wasn't projecting her feelings. This was the best day she'd had in a long time.

She smiled back, feeling relaxed. For a few minutes she'd forgotten to be self-conscious, forgotten to be nervous, forgotten to be worried. It felt good not to worry. She wasn't over-thinking things, she wasn't creating concerns. Despite the fact that the crowds were building up, her earlier nerves had eased. She felt safe with Damien. He seemed to have the ability to create a wall that surrounded the three of them and Jonty and didn't allow the outside world to intrude.

'Get the tiger,' Summer instructed, before Abi could answer.

'Why the tiger?' Damien asked.

'It's got the same eyes as Abi.'

He looked back at Abi then asked to see the toy. He took the tiger with its amber glass eyes and held it beside Abi's head, looking from the glass eyes into hers.

'So it does,' Damien agreed as he held her gaze, and Abi felt the rest of the world dissolve into a haze around her as his dark eyes looked deep inside her. Could he see her reaction? Could he see how happy she was? How confused?

She dropped her gaze and reached for the toy and tucked it under her arm. She couldn't continue to stare at him, afraid she would say or do something she'd regret, like step forward to touch him.

'Thank you,' she said, but her words seemed inadequate to express her feelings. She would remember this day for ever and she knew that if she had nothing else, this tiger would always remind her of today. The first day in six months where she'd felt able to breathe, to relax, to forget her worries. It would remind her of the person she could be; it would inspire her to get over the past, to recover; and it would remind her of Damien and Summer long after they were gone from her life.

She couldn't imagine being part of them for ever. They didn't need her but she was starting to think she needed them. They were saving her, making her feel safe, whole and normal.

She was staring at him with her incredible amber eyes and he knew he would never forget this day.

'It was my pleasure,' he replied.

She was still wearing his jacket. It swamped her tiny frame and made her look vulnerable. She was beautiful but damaged and brought out all his protective instincts. She put out a distress call that he had to answer. He was a sucker for anyone who needed protection. Having someone to protect or care for, like his father had done for his mother, was what it was all about. It made him feel strong, valuable and worthy, and he liked those feelings. He liked feeling needed.

CHAPTER SEVEN

ABI WAS PLEASED to get to work on Monday. She was
feeling overwhelmed, not physically but emotionally.
Her emotions were swamping her and her head was
full of conflicting thoughts about Damien. She wanted
to trust him but she knew it was because she was attracted to him, and she really couldn't afford to be. It
broke all her rules.

But she had to admit she had enjoyed the day at the
pier. She'd felt self-conscious at first about spending the
day with Damien, but he and Summer had relaxed her
and entertained her to the point that she'd forgotten to
be worried, forgotten to be nervous about the crowds.
It had felt like the type of Sunday thousands of normal
families might enjoy and she had liked that feeling. It
was something she'd never had. She had almost been
able to pretend they were one of those families.

But they were not.

Perhaps she needed to think of any time spent with
Damien and Summer as therapy. It had certainly made
her feel good yesterday. She'd felt confident, she'd felt
safe and she had coped with situations that she'd never
imagined she would be able to face again. She had en-

joyed herself. But Damien was still a colleague. It would be prudent to be careful.

She needed to be at work so she was forced to think about other things, things that mattered, like her patients.

She headed for Dylan's room. He was due to have his dressings changed for the first time following the skin grafts to his arms so she needed to be there. She needed a dose of reality. This was her life. Her work. And work was something she could handle. She was trained for this and it didn't require anything extra of her personally. She could cope with work but she couldn't cope with her feelings for Damien or his daughter.

The pull towards them was strong. They were magnetic. Hypnotising. Was it them or was it the idea of them? A family unit but not quite? Something was missing for them, she could feel it. She recognised it because something was missing for her too, but was she living in a fantasy world? Was she kidding herself if she thought she could be the answer for them and vice versa? Why would they need her? No one ever had.

She gloved and gowned and straightened her shoulders as she tied a mask over her nose and mouth before entering Dylan's room. Ellen had been nursing Dylan and she had everything ready and waiting for Abi.

She greeted Dylan's mother, who was pacing at his bedside, waiting anxiously and hoping for good news. 'Morning, Julie,' she said, doing her best to project confidence.

Abi had one eye on the monitors as she picked up Dylan's chart and flicked through it. 'How's he doing?' she asked Ellen, as Dylan dozed. He'd been kept sedated since the surgery as it was important to keep him as still as possible to protect his arms from rubbing or pressure.

'He's doing well. Obs are all good. Temperature normal,' Ellen replied.

A normal temperature was encouraging.

'All right, let's take a look.'

Ellen pushed the trolley closer to the bed as Abi spoke to Dylan's mum. 'We'll change the dressings on his arms this morning. You're welcome to stay while we do this but don't expect the skin on his arms to look normal. Even though I have transplanted normal, healthy skin, it needs time to attach and for the blood supply to be restored.'

Abi and Ellen worked together to remove the bandages. Most came away easily and there was only one small section that required a little soaking. Abi felt positive. The skin she was revealing was red, indicating that the blood vessels were functioning.

'Vascularisation has started,' she commented, pleased with the outcome. 'It's looking good.'

'What about his thighs?' Julie queried.

'The dressings on the donor site will remain on for another few days. His thighs are likely to be more uncomfortable due to the exposed nerve endings, but I will start to lighten his sedation.' She turned to address Ellen. 'Keep the antibiotics running for now.'

'When do you think he might be able to come home?' Julie asked.

'Do you have somewhere to live?' Abi realised she had no idea how badly their house had been damaged in the fire.

'He'll have to share a bedroom with his younger brother but the house is liveable.'

'You should expect him to stay with us for another week but I'll review that in a few days' time and give you a more definite answer then.'

'Will I need anything special when he does come home?'

'We will go through all of that with you before he's discharged. He will need physical therapy but I will get Grace Watson, she's our resident physio, to speak to you before Dylan leaves and she or I will also organise a visit for you from a nurse or occupational therapist to organise any aids he might need. We've got time. The main thing is that he rests, stays relatively still and has time to heal,' Abi explained, as she signed off on Dylan's notes before returning to her office to get the rest of her day under way. She was consulting today. She had four new patients and she wanted a chance to read through their referrals before the appointments.

She sat at her desk, booted up her computer and scanned the list of names in her diary. One jumped off the screen at her. It was the first name on the list but that wasn't what had caught her attention. She recognised this name.

Nicolette Farrington.

It couldn't be.

The name was familiar but surely it couldn't be her.

Abi's heart was racing and she could feel a lump lodge in her throat, but she wasn't quite sure what the lump was. It could be so many things. Fear. Apprehension. Panic.

Nicolette Farrington.

Mark had been a Farrington. He'd had two daughters—Nikki and Natasha.

Abi closed her eyes and took a deep breath as she

tried to stem the rising tide of panic. The words that had been printed on his memorial card flashed across the back of her eyelids.

Devoted husband of Tanya.
Loving father of Nikki and Natasha.

How many Nicolette Farringtons could there be in California? In LA?

She clicked on the patient details, almost reluctant to see what information had been entered. Did she really want to know?

Nicolette's date of birth would make her twenty, which would make her the right age to be Mark's daughter.

Abi was having trouble breathing. Her chest was tight and she could feel a sharp pain between her ribs as she tried to inhale. Apprehension had been replaced by guilt, which joined together with fear and panic. She fought down a wave of nausea as she tried to figure out what to do.

She buzzed her secretary to ask if Nicolette could be moved to Damien's list. She hoped Jennifer wouldn't ask why because what could Abi say?

I have a conflict of interest. She might be the daughter of my ex-lover. My married ex-lover. My dead ex-lover.

But of course Jennifer did ask why. 'Why? Her mother phoned and specifically asked to see you,' she said.

Why would she ask for her by name? Abi wondered. What was going on? What did she know?

'Anyway,' Jennifer continued when Abi stayed mute,

'Damien is in surgery and Nicolette and her mother are already here. They're waiting for you,' she said, as if that ended the issue.

But Abi knew it was far from over. It was only just beginning. Unless it was a different Nicolette Farrington? That was her only hope.

She read through the referral letter on the screen, forcing herself to focus on the important facts and the patient's history as she tried to ignore her nerves. The patient had sustained facial injuries in a motor-vehicle accident three months ago. She had fractured her eye socket, cheekbone, nose and jaw. She had been put back together but the initial focus had been on making sure she survived, not making sure she looked the same as before. And apparently she didn't. This was a reconstructive surgery case and one that Abi would normally be excited about, but it was difficult to be excited when she felt like vomiting.

Still hopeful that she was panicking over nothing, she knew there was only one way to find out. She stood up from her desk, crossed the floor and opened the door.

It was her. *Them.*

There was no mistaking mother and daughter. She recognised them both, even though she had only seen them once before, at Mark's funeral. But they were regular visitors in her dreams and the real-life versions looked identical to her guilt-induced, night-time visions.

They looked up as they heard the door open and Abi felt her heart stop as Mark's pale blue eyes looked directly at her. Nikki's eyes were identical to her father's, the same shape and exactly the same shade, pale blue framed by thick dark lashes. It was like looking at Mark all over again, except a younger, damaged version. Abi hoped her own shock wasn't written all over her face. She wasn't shocked at the damage to Nikki's bone structure but Nikki wouldn't know that. She didn't want her potential patient to think she was shocked by her appearance.

But the surprise of seeing Mark's eyes looking back at her rendered her immobile for a few seconds before she came to her senses. Before she was able to ignore the colour of Nikki's eyes, to ignore the fact that she had dark hair like her father's, although his had been sprinkled with salt and pepper, before she was able to look at the whole person.

This wasn't the girl Abi remembered from the funeral. There were few similarities between this girl and the one she recalled. She had been a pretty girl but the right side of her face looked completely different now. Her facial injuries must have been extensive or perhaps she had simply been badly managed. There was no correlation between the two halves of her face, between right and left. It was as if two different people had been put together to make one. Her face was lopsided, her nose was crooked, her right cheekbone was depressed and her right eye drooped.

Abi began to examine Nikki from a distance, looking at her face shape and bone structure and working out how she could fix her. She forgot about Mark. She forgot about his connection to this young woman. All she saw before her now was a girl who needed her help.

She swallowed her nerves and worries. Her professional mask slipped into place, hiding her own fears and insecurities. 'Nicolette? I'm Dr Thompson. Would you like to come through?'

Abi managed to get through the beginning of the

consultation by sticking to the script. She introduced herself to Nikki's mother, Tanya, Mark's widow, terrified she was going to start making accusations, but Tanya didn't mention Mark and Abi relaxed. She got Nikki's history and made an effort to focus on her; she couldn't afford to dwell on Mark. The sins of the father were not Nikki's fault or her problem.

She made notes about Nikki's medical and surgical management post-accident, listing the issues Nikki reported—difficulty with eating and talking—and her concerns about her appearance. She listened to her say she just wanted to be normal. Abi could relate to that. Some people had external scars, others internal, but in the end everyone just wanted to be accepted, and for a young woman appearance was important. Abi got that and she would do her best to help.

Abi typed Nikki's information into her computer, aware that Tanya was watching her closely. 'Have we met?' she asked.

'No,' Abi answered quickly, almost abruptly, and hoped Tanya didn't hear the strain in her voice. She wasn't telling a lie. Abi had seen them at Mark's funeral but his betrayal had stunned her and she had avoided them. She had left as soon as she'd realised, not wanting to stay until the end, not wanting to make any accidental eye contact with Mark's widow. She'd been terrified her guilt and shame and anger would have been written across her face for anyone to see.

The fear that she'd managed to put to one side after seeing Nikki's name on her list returned with Tanya's question. How had Tanya ended up here, in her consulting room? How had she found her? Was it a simple coincidence or was there more to it? Did she know something she wasn't telling Abi? Was she deliberately stirring the pot?

Abi couldn't ask—to do so would admit she'd known Mark and invite a whole lot of questions she wasn't prepared, or probably equipped, to answer. It was better to feign ignorance. She could treat Nikki without ever having to reveal her connection, her history, with Nikki's father and Tanya's husband.

Did that make her as deceitful as Mark?

No, it didn't. It couldn't. Mark's lies had destroyed Abi but that didn't mean she wanted to do the same to his family. There was no point in saying anything now. There was nothing to be gained. To speak up would only hurt people. Keeping quiet was the best option, the only option, in Abi's mind.

She was aware of Tanya still watching her, studying her closely, and it made her feel uncomfortable. In an attempt to distract her, she moved on to discuss the process for the surgery.

'I will need some time to plan the surgery. I'll need to take measurements and photos of Nikki's face and if you have some photos of Nikki from before the accident that would be helpful. Did my secretary ask you for those when you booked the appointment?'

Tanya nodded and hoisted her handbag onto her lap and pulled out a large envelope. 'I brought some with us.' She passed the envelope to Abi, who shook the photos out onto her desk.

She felt herself go pale as she picked up the first picture. It was a family photo, a snapshot of Tanya, her two daughters and her husband. The resemblance between Nicolette and her father was even more obvious in this picture.

Mark had turned fifty when they had been in Afghanistan. Abi could remember the long weekend they'd had on leave shortly after, the weekend they had spent in Prague, celebrating. This picture must have been taken around the same time, some time in the past twelve months at least. Mark looked just as she remembered him. His dark hair had been greying slightly, starting at the temples where it had turned silver. He had carried a bit of extra weight but had been in great shape. He had looked vital, alive, robust. He didn't look like the Mark she saw in her dreams. This wasn't the Mark who had lain on the ground in the middle of a panicking crowd, bleeding onto the street, or the man whose life had drained out of him while she had tried in vain to save him.

In this photograph, taken when he'd been smiling and his pale blue eyes crinkled at the corners, he looked like a man you would trust. But it just showed that looks could be deceptive, for in reality he had also been a liar and a cheat.

But all that was in the past now. There was no way of bringing him back and she knew she wouldn't want him back now, even if that had been an option. She was done with him. Now she just needed to get his family out of her life too.

She should be able to reconstruct Nicolette's face without too much trouble. Despite everything, she could remember the shape and feel of Mark's face under her fingers. She would be able to restore his daughter's face.

She put the photo down and flicked through the others. Had she spent too long looking at that one? Too long looking at Mark's face instead of at Nikki's? Had she seemed distracted, inattentive, vague? She moved to the other photos—Nikki dressed for a school prom, her yearbook photo, a birthday party, a close-up head shot of her with her sister.

'Can I keep these photos?' she asked.

'What are you going to do with them?'

'I'll make enlarged copies. The more information I can gather, the better the outcome of surgery.'

Tanya nodded. 'So you think you can help?'

'Yes.' Abi's voice was strong, confident.

She printed off a diagram of a face and measured Nikki's features, jotting figures onto the paper record. She was relieved to find that her hands didn't tremble as she measured the width of Nikki's face, the distance between her eyes, the height of her philtrum, and took more photos.

'What happens next?' Nikki asked, as Abi put the camera down.

Now she needed some time. 'I will see you again in a couple of days to go through the plan for the surgery in more detail once I've worked out the best approach, and if you want to go ahead we should be able to schedule the surgery for next week. I'll get my secretary to make a follow-up appointment.'

Abi asked Jennifer to pencil the surgery into her diary and make sure that Damien would be free to assist her before she said goodbye. She could feel a headache starting and would really have liked to lie down somewhere quiet and pull the covers over her head. She needed Jonty's company, or Damien's. Either of them would help to settle her nerves and fears, relieve the tension she could feel building inside her, but she didn't have either of them. And she couldn't seek Damien out. She wouldn't be able to explain her problem. She didn't want to discuss it with him so she stretched her neck and shoulders, took two paracetamol tablets and got on with her day.

Abi had expected to have a few days to pull herself together before she saw Tanya again but it happened sooner than she expected. She was waiting for Damien as they had a meeting scheduled to discuss Nikki's surgery further when Jennifer buzzed her office.

'Mrs Farrington is here,' Jennifer said.

'Nikki's appointment isn't until tomorrow,' Abi replied.

'She knows that. Nikki isn't with her. Mrs Farrington wants to know if she can have a minute of your time. She has some more photos for you.'

Nikki's surgery was scheduled for next week. She didn't need to see Tanya, there was absolutely no reason to see her, but she found herself saying yes.

She carried a fistful of photos in with her. Photos Abi assumed were of Nikki, and she wondered why she couldn't have left them with Jennifer, but as Tanya marched across to her desk and fanned the pictures out across the surface, Abi realised why. These weren't photos of Nikki. They were photos of Mark.

And Abi.

'I knew I'd seen you before,' Tanya said.

Abi clenched her fists at her sides to stop herself from reaching out and picking up the pictures. 'I worked with your husband,' she replied. Her heart was hammering in her chest and it made her voice jump in her throat.

Tanya spread the photos out further, shuffling through the assortment until she found the one she wanted. She pulled out a shot that showed Mark with his arm around Abi's shoulders. She was beaming up at him, looking like a woman in love. It had been taken on their weekend's leave in Prague, a belated celebration of Mark's fiftieth birthday. At the time Abi had thought it was the most beautiful city, the most beautiful place, in the world but it had all been lies. Abi couldn't believe that woman in the photo was her. It had only been taken nine months ago but she had been so naive back then. She had grown up a lot since and now she didn't even recognise this woman.

'Let's be honest, shall we?' Tanya said. 'This was more than a working relationship. A lot more.'

'Where did you get these?' Abi's voice was wobbling and her hands were shaking. She kept them clenched at her sides but now it was in an attempt to stop the tremors.

'They were sent to me with Mark's things. All neatly boxed up. Photos of my husband with another woman.'

Of course, Abi realised, his personal effects would have been sent to his next of kin. His wife. The one Abi hadn't known anything about.

Why had she insisted on printing these photos and giving them to Mark?

She knew why. She'd wanted him to put them in his office or his room but he never had. She'd wanted to feel like they were a proper couple, like she was going to be part of his life when they returned to the States. After all, that was what he had promised her, and she had believed him. Despite the fact that he'd insisted on keeping their relationship secret—he'd told her that, because of his position as her CO, he didn't think it was right to parade their relationship, and she had agreed. She'd had the future to look forward to so she could wait. But then she'd found out his promises had been empty ones. At the funeral she'd realised why he had wanted secrecy.

After he had died she hadn't thought about looking for the photos, destroying them. She'd been too upset to consider things like that. She'd had her own copies and she hadn't considered that Mark's personal belongings would be sent back to his family. She hadn't thought he'd had a wife. Daughters, yes, but he'd told her he was divorced. And she had believed him. She'd had no reason not to.

'Were you having an affair with my husband?' Tanya asked.

Abi didn't know what to say. 'We were having a relationship,' she admitted. It seemed pointless to deny that under the circumstances. 'But I didn't know he was married. I didn't know it was an affair. I didn't know about you until his funeral.'

Abi had seen Tanya and her daughters at the front of the church but had still assumed that Tanya was the ex-wife. Until she had opened the memorial card and seen what it so clearly stated.

Devoted husband of Tanya.
Loving father of Nikki and Natasha.

Mark hadn't been divorced. Mark hadn't been planning on making a life with her. He had still been married.

She had left the funeral before it had finished. She had fled almost before it had started. She would never have attended in the first place if she had known. She'd felt embarrassed, humiliated and ashamed.

Abi picked up the photo of her and Mark in Prague. Looking at her picture, it would be obvious to anyone how she felt about Mark but Mark, other than the fact he had an arm around her shoulder, looked completely unaffected. Abi could just be a silly colleague. What had made Tanya suspicious?

'How did you know?' she asked.

'You're in all these photos. And I know Mark. You weren't the first and I would guess you wouldn't have been the last,' she continued. 'I knew Mark had affairs.'

'You knew?'

'I didn't know about you specifically, you were just another in a long line, I expect, and I had learnt to turn a blind eye.'

'Didn't it bother you?'

Tanya shrugged. 'As far as I was aware, his affairs were always conducted when he was away from home. I figured as long as it didn't affect the girls I could put up with it. I could have asked for a divorce but I didn't, for the sake of the girls. It was easier just to get on with my life and ignore what he got up to when he was away. He always came home to us and I always let him. That was my choice.'

Tanya didn't sound angry or upset. If Abi had to describe how she sounded, she would have said resigned, but it was Abi who was surprised. Of everything she had expected, imagined, this sense of resignation wasn't it.

'Only this time he didn't come home.' The words were out of Abi's mouth before she could stop them. Harsh words, she spoke the truth, but she hadn't meant to voice her opinion.

'He should have been more careful.' Tanya reached

out her hand and her fingers traced the line of Mark's face in one of the photos that lay on the desk. 'I guess he didn't expect to die over there.'

Abi didn't tell her that he *would* have expected that. They all had. Tanya didn't need to hear that. She had loved her husband—that was clearly obvious. She didn't need to hear the details.

'I couldn't save him,' Abi said in reply. 'I'm sorry.'

'You were there?'

She nodded.

'What happened?'

'What did the army tell you?' Abi wasn't sure if she could bear to vocalise the truth of that fateful day. Talking to Damien was one thing but it was something quite different to tell Mark's widow the cold, hard facts. She didn't want her to have the same nightmares she had. Someone who was emotionally invested in Mark didn't need to hear the details. She didn't need the truth.

'Not much,' Tanya replied. 'They said it was a bomb and that he died instantly. But if you were there...' Her voice trailed off and Abi knew what she was thinking. She was wondering how Abi had survived.

Abi knew the army would have been as kind as they could when they'd informed Mark's family of his death. She agreed there was no need to go into the details of his suffering—to tell Tanya that Mark had died in her arms, that he'd been unable to speak and unable to breathe. That she had listened to his last breath, had seen it bubble out of his chest and leave his lips. She nodded. 'That's what happened.'

'But you were all right?'

Did Tanya think that was unfair? Abi couldn't blame her but she couldn't argue with the facts. Abi had survived, although not without scars, both physical and emotional. 'I was injured but not badly. Mark was nearer to the explosion.'

Tanya sat on the chair in front of Abi's desk and Abi could almost see the strength seeping out of her. She had obviously been fighting to hold it all together. Was it still for the sake of her daughters or was it her way of coping? Abi didn't know but that made her think of the reason Tanya was even in her office in the first place. Nicolette.

Considering how things stood now, would they still choose her as Nicolette's surgeon? She imagined this might be enough to persuade them otherwise. How would she explain that to Damien? He had agreed to assist her with the surgery—how could she tell him that the surgery wouldn't be going ahead because she'd had an affair with the patient's father?

Her first concern wasn't how she would explain this to James and Freya, how she would tell them that she had lost them business, but how she would break the news to Damien. What would he think?

'Do you want me to find someone else to do Nikki's surgery?' Abi asked. There was no delicate way of asking that question.

'*Can* you do it?'

'Yes.'

'Will your feelings about Mark or me or Nikki affect your process?'

Abi's only feelings towards Mark now were anger and betrayal. She knew she needed to let that go and she was in the process of doing so, but she would make sure her feelings would not affect Nikki's care. She was a professional, an expert. At least in a surgical sense she was, even if all other areas of her life were a shambles, this was something she knew she could do and do well. Medicine was all she had. 'Not at all,' she said. 'I always give one hundred per cent. What happened between Mark and me has nothing to do with Nikki. She will get the best possible care and outcome I can give her.' This would be her way of making amends.

Tanya was nodding. 'Good. I don't want to find someone else. Nikki liked you. She felt comfortable and you were recommended to us. We are still struggling to come to terms with Mark's death and Nikki's accident has just made matters worse. I'm used to being on my own and taking care of the girls, but there's a lot more going on than normal.

'Things have changed. In the past I always knew that Mark would come home or I could pick up the phone and discuss issues with him. I can't do that any more. I have to be able to manage on my own. If I can get one thing back on track, perhaps it will help us to feel as if we will be okay. This is important to Nikki. I don't think she will cope with another setback. The girls are all I have left. Everything I do, everything I have ever done has been for them.'

Tanya had straightened her shoulders as she'd spoken, as she prepared herself to fight on her daughter's behalf, and listening to her made Abi wish she'd had someone who would have fought like that for her.

'I'll do my best for her,' Abi promised.

Tanya was a strong woman and, ironically, Abi thought she could probably take a leaf out of her book. She could learn to stare adversity in the face, to not back down, to not be afraid.

But, then, Tanya had something to fight for. She had her daughters.

What did *she* have?

Abi saw Tanya out of her office. She opened the door and found Damien poised on the threshold. In the shock of Tanya's disclosure Abi had forgotten about their meeting. She turned around and Damien followed. To her dismay, the first thing she saw when she turned were Tanya's photos spread across her desk. She hadn't thought to pack them away, she hadn't known what to do with them. She didn't want to keep them, she didn't even want to look at them, but to sweep them off her desk and into a drawer would only draw Damien's attention to them. She would have to stack them in a pile and get rid of them later, but before she could gather them together Damien had reached over and picked one up. It was one of Abi in uniform.

Abi held her breath while he looked it over.

He pointed at Mark. 'Who's this?'

'Mark Farrington.'

'Your commanding officer?'

Abi nodded.

'You were in a relationship with him?'

Abi felt the colour drain from her face. Was it obvious to everyone?

She nodded again.

'So Nicolette Farrington is a relative?'

'His daughter.'

'You know her?'

'No. I'd never met her until two days ago. The referral is just a coincidence. I don't know his family. They don't know me.'

'His family?' Nicolette's file was on Abi's desk.

Damien flicked it open and picked up another photo. The family photo. It clearly showed Mark and Tanya's hands. Their wedding rings. 'He's married?'

'Seems he was,' Abi replied. 'Not that he shared that information with me.'

'You didn't know?'

She shook her head. 'I found out at his funeral.' She tried to explain. 'Finding out that I'd been in a relationship with someone else's husband compounded my PTSD. The guilt over Mark's death and the affair in addition to the stress from the bombing incident was the last straw.' Abi wasn't sure if Damien would believe her but it was suddenly extremely important to her that he did. She wanted, needed, him to trust in her.

Damien put the photos back on her desk. He turned the one with her in it face down, very slowly and very deliberately. What was he thinking? Did he believe her or was he going to torture her over the affair?

'Does his wife know?' he asked.

Abi nodded. 'She gave me the photos.'

'Do you still think it's a good idea to take Nikki on as a patient?'

'Yes. I can do this and I think it will be amazing. We can transform Nikki physically, improve her function and her aesthetics and restore her confidence. I know what it's like to have your confidence completely destroyed. Mark's lies did that to me.'

'Will you be able to put that behind you when you operate on his daughter?'

Abi nodded. 'I'm angry with Mark for taking advantage of me and angry with myself for being so gullible, but I'm not angry with Nikki. This is my chance to make amends for what I did, albeit unknowingly, but it's a form of redemption. I'll feel better if I can make up for my mistakes.'

'Are you doing this for Nikki or for yourself?'

'For both of us.' Her own self-confidence had been seriously dented by Mark's lies but even if her personal life was a wreck, at least she had her work and despite Mark's behaviour she would do her best for his daughter. 'I have no intention of failing to do my best for any of my patients, and that includes Nikki. But I need your help.'

'Are you sure you can do this?'

Abi nodded.

In Damien's opinion that was a big statement to make and he wasn't convinced that he believed her but, despite that, he could feel himself wanting to help her. But he hesitated before he committed himself to her cause. He needed to examine why he felt this urge to help. Was it because he felt she would need support? There was no doubt she was qualified to perform the surgery but did he think she was emotionally capable? Did he want to help because he thought he might need to pick up the pieces?

He knew she had been taken advantage of. She'd been mistreated, abused, emotionally if not physically. His protective instincts were strong at the best of times but something about Abi made them even more reactive. Abi wasn't manipulative, like his ex. She was altruistic and because he could sense the goodness in her he knew he would give her anything she asked for. Including this.

'All right,' he told her. 'I will help you.'

'Hi, have you got a minute?'

Damien was standing in her doorway. She was getting used to him popping in and out on a regular basis. She was getting used to his dark good looks, the shine in the depths of his dark eyes and the spontaneous smile that was often so unexpected but always made her spirits lift.

'Sure.'

'How are you coping?' he asked.

'I'm good,' she replied, and realised that she spoke the truth. She was feeling good with herself for the first time in months. Guilt about the affair had compounded her PTSD and exacerbated her symptoms, but finding out that Tanya knew about Mark's behaviour and that Abi hadn't been his only dalliance had lessened her guilt. Her conscience had eased and so had her stress.

'Are you busy on Sunday afternoon?'

'Sunday? No.' She'd assumed Damien's question would have been work-related but she had no plans. She never had plans. 'Why?'

'I've been invited to the film industry awards.'

'Wow! Really? By whom?' He really did live a different life from her. She couldn't believe she had even dared imagine after their day at the pier that she could be a part of it.

'One of my patients has been nominated for Best Supporting Actor. He had oral cancer, a squamous cell carcinoma with secondaries in his jaw. I reconstructed his mandible and he was able to return to acting, and he's invited me on Sunday as a thank-you.'

'Would you like me to look after Summer for you?'

'Summer?' Damien shook his head. 'No. I wanted to know if you would like to come with me.'

'To the awards ceremony? Me? Why would you want to take me?'

'Who else would you suggest?' He was laughing now, the little creases in the corners of his eyes bringing life to the smooth planes of his face.

Freya, Mila. She couldn't think of any single girls. And if she could have, would she want him to choose them over her?

'I want to take you,' he said, making Abi wish everything in life was that simple. 'I thought you might enjoy it. I know you said you're coping with the pressure of operating on Nikki and I know you want to go ahead with that and I accept that is your choice—' Abi knew he had reservations about the surgery. He had told her he was worried that it would increase her stress levels and possibly exacerbate her PTSD, but Abi had insisted she could manage. Work was the one thing in her life that she felt she had some control over. '—but you've seemed a bit quiet, a bit preoccupied, and I thought this would get your mind off things. Off Mark. So, if you're going to insist on operating on Nikki and taking on all the stress that is going along with that, I'm going to insist that you have some down time. And the film industry awards are it.'

She would admit, but only to herself, that she had been thinking more about Mark over the past few days, because of Nikki, but she felt she was coping. And undertaking a complicated surgery seemed less stressful to her than negotiating LA crowds.

'Thank you, it's a lovely idea and I'm sure it would be amazing but I don't know if I can do it.'

'I know you're not busy.'

'It's not that. It's the crowds I'm worried about. They're always huge.'

'It's okay. I've checked it out, I'll organise a limousine, we'll get dropped at the red carpet. Don't worry,' he added when he saw her expression, 'we'll be there way before the celebrities. We have to be early, but it will be safe—security is always tight. I won't let anything happen to you.'

Abi emerged from the bathroom after reapplying her lipstick. She wanted to pinch herself. She couldn't believe she had just been to the film industry awards and was now at an awards after-party, rubbing shoulders with celebrities and stars that she'd watched on screen for years. Despite Damien insisting she would be safe, she had been terribly nervous when they had arrived at the theatre. She'd opened and closed her fingers repeatedly, searching for the reassuring feel of Jonty's fur, but he hadn't been beside her. But Damien had been, and he'd sensed her nervousness and taken her hand as they'd walked the red carpet, but that had only led to a whole different level of nervousness.

His touch had sent her hormones into overdrive but at least she'd forgotten to worry about her safety. All she'd been able to think of had been Damien, and once seated in the darkened theatre, still hand in hand, she'd been able to ignore the size of the audience by focusing on him. He anchored her and made her feel safe and eventually she'd relaxed, but she was even better now that they were in a smaller crowd and a private setting.

She saw Damien across the room. He was talking to Tony, his patient who had invited them to the ceremony and who had walked away with the award for Best Supporting Actor. In a room full of beautiful people Damien was still noticeable. Tall, dark and movie-star handsome, he was turning heads in a space that was crammed with stunning people.

He saw her and waved her over and she picked her way carefully through the crowd.

'Okay, pretty lady, photo time.' Tony's voice was raspy from years of smoking. Which he said was fortunate as the surgery had made it even raspier but no one really noticed. It was his trademark.

He held his prized statuette in his hand and offered it to Abi as he manoeuvred her between Damien and himself. 'You hold it. It'll make a great pic for your social media posts.'

Abi wasn't on social media but she wasn't about to admit that. She was sure that no one here would understand her reasons. She knew that many of the stars saw social media as a source of free publicity and that publicity was their life blood, but social media didn't have the same appeal to her.

She took the little gold statue from Tony, surprised he was willing to let it go just hours after receiving it, but she wasn't going to argue. This was a once-in-a-lifetime opportunity for her.

Damien pulled his mobile phone from his suit pocket and handed it to a passing celebrity. Abi couldn't believe that this young actress who had been nominated for an award was taking her picture.

Tony was on her right, Damien on her left as she posed for the photo, and the statuette glowed golden against the emerald-green silk of the dress she'd borrowed from Freya.

Damien wrapped his arm around her waist and the heat of his hand burned through the fabric of her dress. The dress was cut low at the back and she could feel his forearm against her spine, skin on skin. The award was heavy in her hand, her knees were weak and her heart fluttered in her chest.

The instant the photo had been taken she returned the statuette to Tony, afraid she would drop it.

Tony checked the photo. Although he was almost thirty years older than Abi, approaching sixty, he had a reputation as a heart-throb and once again Abi was conscious of the fact that these people made a living as much out of their looks as their talent. She was self-conscious about her own appearance so his comment caught her by surprise. 'You look gorgeous, Abigail. If Damien hadn't already snatched you up I'd invite you to—'

Abi opened her mouth to correct his assumption, to tell him she and Damien weren't a couple, when she felt Damien's hand on her arm and she stopped.

'She's off limits, Tony. Besides, you've got your prize already tonight.'

'True, very true.' Tony laughed. 'Point taken. Go and have some fun.' He kissed Abi's cheek and said, 'Enjoy the party.'

'We will,' Damien said, as he snared them both a glass of French champagne from a passing waitress.

'Why did you let him think we were a couple?' Abi asked as Damien handed her a glass.

'Tony is a notorious charmer,' he said. 'No one is off limits and I didn't think you'd want to be subjected to that. I didn't think he was your type.'

What was her type? She didn't know.

They sipped champagne and watched the crowd. It was an incredible evening to be a part of, even if she did feel like an outsider. Even though she didn't believe in them, it felt a little bit like a fairytale. She could pretend she was playing a part in a movie—only as an extra, but it was a fun feeling being able to reinvent herself. Tonight she could be carefree, happy, loved. Tonight she could be anything she wanted.

The band began playing an old Frank Sinatra song. 'Shall we dance?' Damien asked.

He guided her around the dance floor with his hand on her back and his lips in her hair. She'd imagined he would be a fabulous dancer and she wasn't disappointed. They danced chest to chest and Abi closed her eyes and pretended that she belonged at the party, pretended that she belonged in his arms as she continued with her fantasy of reinvention. Tonight she was a girl who could have anything her heart desired.

His hand moved lower to rest in the small of her back. She could feel each fingertip against her skin and his breath was soft on her ear. She let the occasion and the company seduce her as she imagined Damien kissing her. Tried to imagine how he would taste.

She was in a bubble, their own small world. Nothing existed except the two of them. Her senses had shut down, other than the most basic. All she could think about was sex, desire, want and need. And Damien.

Tonight she was a girl who could have anything her heart desired. And she desired Damien.

CHAPTER EIGHT

SHE SAT BESIDE him in the limousine. Their thighs were touching and the heat from his body scorched her skin and warmed her insides.

A bottle of champagne was chilling in an ice bucket. Damien reached for it and poured them each a glass. The champagne was cold and the sharp contrast between the coldness of the drink and the temperature of her body made her catch her breath.

Damien sipped his drink, drawing her attention to his lips. She imagined leaning forward, pressing her lips to his, tasting him, as she'd been longing to do all evening, but before she could decide whether to take that chance the driver had turned into her driveway and pulled up behind Damien's car, which was where he had left it after dropping Summer off with Irma and George for a sleepover.

He took her glass from her hand and put it down in the limousine. He picked up the bottle as the driver opened Abi's door.

'Do you have champagne flutes?' he asked.

She had been wondering if she was brave enough to invite him in when he took the initiative. Had he read her mind or seen the question, the desire, in her eyes?

She swallowed. 'I'm sure I can find something appro-
priate,' she said. She had no idea what was in her cupboards but did it matter if she didn't have champagne
flutes? She would drink out of jam jars if it meant pro-
longing the evening.

Damien followed her inside and she could sense his
eyes watching the tightening of her butt as she climbed
the stairs. She searched the kitchen cupboards and found
two fluted glasses. Damien filled them before propos-
ing a toast.

'Here's to golden nights,' he said.

She closed her eyes as she sipped her drink. She
could picture the waves of desire that surrounded her to
form a kaleidoscope of colour. She could smell the bub-
bles, as well as Damien's fresh citrus scent. It enveloped
her, surrounded her, cushioned her and kept her safe.

She opened her eyes to find him watching her. His
gaze was unwavering and she could see desire in the
dark depths of his eyes. She felt her temperature rise
as a flush stole over her cheeks and anticipation burned
brightly inside her. She couldn't breathe. His gaze was
so intense it felt as if the room lacked oxygen, as if it
was being burnt up in his gaze. She parted her lips to
take a breath. Her lips were dry so she licked them with
the tip of her tongue.

Damien groaned, giving in to his desire, giving in to
hers. He wrapped an arm around her back, pulled her
to him and kissed her hard. He tasted of champagne,
of late nights and silent promises.

She waited for her nerves to raise the alarm, to ask
her what she thought she was doing, but the anxiety
didn't come, the alarm didn't sound. She wanted this,

she needed this. There was no fear. In Damien's arms she felt safe. Beautiful. Special. Desirable.

Nothing else mattered.

There was nothing else.

She reached one hand behind his head, holding him to her as she kissed him back. His tongue was warm in her mouth. His hands were warm on her skin. Every inch of her was on fire, consumed with desire. She felt his fingers on her arm, could feel them tracing a line up to her shoulder, across her collarbone to the hollow at the base of her throat, where she felt his thumb dip into the little dimple. She couldn't breathe, she'd forgotten how.

Abi needed to breathe.

She pulled away and he lifted his hand, releasing her from his touch. She almost begged him not to as she didn't want him to let her go.

'Are you okay?' he asked.

She nodded, unable to speak.

His dark gaze moved lower, over her breasts. How could such dark eyes hold such heat? Such intensity? She held her breath, trying to stop the rise and fall of her breasts, but still her nipples peaked in response to his gaze burning through the thin fabric of her dress. She could feel the moisture between her legs as her body responded to his gaze devouring her. He wasn't laying a finger on her now and yet she felt ready to self-combust. A look, a glance, a smile was all it would take for her to melt under him.

'Do you want to stop?'

'No.' Her voice was breathless. 'I want you to make love to me.'

She didn't need to ask twice. With one arm he

scooped her up and held her against his chest, pressing her to him, as he carried her into her bedroom.

He lowered her to the bed before shrugging out of his jacket. He tugged at one end of his bow tie, pulling it undone and tossing it onto the chair at her bedside. He eased himself over her, supporting himself on his elbows. She reached up and ran her hands over his biceps, feeling his strength, marvelling at the firmness within him. His breath was coming fast now, she could hear it and feel it as it hit the bare skin of her shoulders and neck, but he didn't move. How could he hold himself so still? He was poised to move forward, to take this to the next level, but somehow he held his position. He was in no hurry. How could he be so calm when desire threatened to consume her?

The waiting was exquisite agony. A delicious sense of anticipation battled with the desire to have him take her now, right now. She arched her hips up towards him, pushing herself against his groin, and was rewarded when she felt his matching desire, hard and firm, straining against his trousers.

She breathed out on a sigh as she let her knees fall open and wrapped her legs around him, pulling him closer, pulling him down against her. She heard him groan and he lowered his body until it covered the length of her. She wanted this. She wanted to feel his weight on her, she needed to know this was real.

Every cell of her body tingled, she could feel each one straining, alive with the possibilities of what was to come. Her expectations were almost painful, her reaction intense.

He reached for her, ending her suspense. His lips were on her ear lobe, soft and warm, his breath in her ear. He kissed her neck and then his lips covered hers and she melted into him and let him consume her.

His fingers skimmed over her nipples, hard and peaked. He swept the strap of her dress from her shoulder and exposed her left breast to the cool air. His thumb brushed over her nipple, teasing, tantalising. She cried out as a wave of desire washed over her and a bolt of heat scorched through her, sweeping from her nipple to her groin in a searing flash.

His lips left a trail of hot spots from her lips to her throat and collarbone until finally he took her breast in his mouth, rolling his tongue over the taut flesh until Abi thought she might come then and there. But she didn't want it to end. Not yet. Maybe not ever. She wanted to feel him, to touch him, to arouse him too.

Her fingers found the buttons of his shirt and she undid them, one by one, until she could run her hand over his chest. His warm skin was firm but soft under her fingertips. She pulled his shirt from his body as his mouth continued to tease her nipple, sucking and licking. He cupped her breast in his hand and ran his thumb over the peaked bud, making her moan. She arched her back, offering herself to him, and he took one breast in his mouth again, sucking hard, and she almost exploded in his arms.

She ran her index finger from his sternum down along the line separating his abdominal muscles, following the line of dark hair that led below his waistband. She concentrated on him, wanting to extend the pleasure, wanting to share the delight. She unbuckled his belt and snapped open the button on his trousers, unzipping his fly and pushing his trousers low on his hips. His erection strained against the fabric of his boxer shorts. She pushed them out of the way and ran her hand over his shaft, which was strong and thick, and she felt it rise to meet her. He groaned and the sound of his arousal urged her on.

His hand ran up her thigh and the soft folds of her dress fell away with his touch. His fingers met the elastic of her underwear and slid under the lace. Abi let her legs fall apart again, opening herself to him, giving herself to him, and she bit back a cry of desire as his fingers slid inside her. She was slick and wet, throbbing. His thumb found her centre and she gasped as his touch took her to the edge.

But she didn't want it this way. She wanted to share the experience. She wanted all of him and she wanted him to have all of her. She let go of him to quickly pull her dress over her head, and now she lay naked before him. His dark eyes roamed over her body, setting her on fire with his gaze.

She wanted to feel him inside her. She wanted them to be joined together. She lifted her hips and reached behind him, holding his hips, cupping his buttocks, to pull him close. Her knees were bent and she arched her back as she fitted him to her like pieces of a jigsaw.

She gave herself to him and he claimed all of her.

She sighed as he thrust into her, filling her, consuming her as they became one.

This was dangerous, *she* was dangerous, Damien thought as he felt himself losing control. Everything else in his life was forgotten as Abi took over his senses. He wanted to go slowly, he wanted to savour the moment, he wanted time to commit it all to memory, but he couldn't resist her. He couldn't fight it. He was only a man, a powerless man, and he could feel himself being swept away. The world ceased to exist except for Abi.

There was nothing else.

Nothing else that mattered.

He felt her hand on his chest, felt it brush over one nipple, felt another surge of blood to his groin. He breathed her name and that was the last coherent thought he had. Her legs wrapped around his waist, pinning him to her. She pushed her hips against his and his resistance crumbled.

She tilted her hips and fitted him to her. He heard his own guttural moan as he thrust into her, filling her, claiming her for his own. He couldn't hold back, he couldn't resist, and when he heard her call his name it pushed him further.

There was nothing gentle in their lovemaking. It was fuelled by pure desire. Desperate, all-consuming desire.

He thrust into her again. Up and down he moved, faster and faster, harder and stronger, and she met each thrust. She arched her back and held him close with her legs, opening herself to him, offering herself to him.

He buried himself deep inside her and when he felt her shudder and come undone he came with her. They climaxed together and when they were completely spent he gathered her to him, holding her close, reluctant to let her go as he savoured this next moment, as they lay in each other's arms, slick with sweat and breathing hard.

She had blown his mind. She was bold and confident. *This* was the Abi who had been hiding, the one he had known was in there somewhere, the one who had been swamped by trauma and stress. He was finally piecing her together. Bit by bit he was getting to know her and he knew now he could bring her back, resurrect her, restore her. All she needed was love, a connection, some-one to nourish her. He could be that man.

He wanted to be that man.

Abi woke to the smell of fresh coffee. She had slept well, without nightmares. She couldn't remember the last time she had slept soundly all night. Actually, she could. It had been last week when she'd fallen asleep in Damien's arms. She'd had two good nights' sleep in the past six months since Mark had died and both of those nights she had spent with Damien.

He was standing by her bed, holding a mug of hot coffee. She could get used to waking up like this.

'Good morning,' he said, as he put the coffee beside her bed and kissed her.

She could definitely get used to this.

'Good morning.' She smiled.

'Do you mind if I have a shower here? I need to col-lect Summer from Irma and George and it will save me some time if I don't have to go and come back.'

'Of course. There are fresh towels in the bathroom cupboard,' she replied. She rolled lazily over onto her stomach and watched as he disappeared into the bath-room.

He showered and returned bare-chested with one of her fluffy white towels wrapped around his waist. He dropped the towel and grinned when her eyes went straight to his groin. He was certainly impressive, lack-ing nothing she needed in that department, and she was disappointed to know there was no time to take advan-tage of his attributes.

'Another time, my lady,' he said, as he bent to pick up his trousers.

Like her when she had slept at his house, he only had yesterday's clothes to wear but there was not the same sense of shame for a man to put on yesterday's clothes. Without the jacket and bow tie his suit became just a pair of trousers and a shirt, and once he got to work and put a white coat over the top no one would be any the wiser.

She was happy to lie in bed and watch him get ready. It felt comfortable, easy; it didn't feel as if they'd only spent one night together but before they could talk about what happened next he was gone. Off to collect Summer and get on with his day, and Abi had no idea what he was thinking.

A fortnight went past in the blink of an eye. It was amazing how quickly time flew when every minute was filled. Between work and spending time with Damien and Summer, Abi had never been as busy, exhausted or happy.

Nikki's operation had gone well and Dylan had been discharged following his skin-graft surgery. She was pleased with the results of Nikki's op, even though it was early days. Her face was still swollen but Abi could already see the improvement made by the repaired bone structure. Nikki had some hip pain from where they had taken the bone graft but that was to be expected and Abi felt confident that everything had gone according to plan.

Damien's attentions were also helping to restore her confidence. Spending time with him was helping to make her whole again and she was feeling more positive than she had in a long time. She could see light at the end of the dark tunnel now, thanks to Damien.

They spent the weekends together, with Summer as their chaperone. Abi played tour guide but when Summer went to bed they got their adult time. Life was good and the sex was amazing but there had been no discussion about where they were headed. Damien hadn't raised the topic and Abi wasn't about to instigate it. She didn't want to formalise their liaison, afraid of jeopardising her happiness. Every relationship she'd ever had had ended badly, and she was superstitious and fearful enough not to want to have that discussion. She didn't want to legitimise what they had for fear that something would go wrong. She didn't want to be the one to cause the bubble to burst. She didn't want to risk ruining the fairytale she had only just started to believe could exist.

She desperately wanted to give her heart away, she wanted to find someone who might want to look after it, but she was terrified of the consequences. She was terrified that she would end up with a bruised and damaged heart and that some tragedy would befall Damien. It was better to keep things uncomplicated. It was better to just keep quiet.

But despite her reservations she was looking forward to another weekend. Their weekdays were hectic, between their work commitments, taking care of Jonty, her appointments with her psychologist and Damien's hands-on role as single dad to Summer, it didn't leave them with much time for romance and Abi had already learned to hold out for Friday night. She was enjoying having someone to share her time with, someone to spend weekends with, and she smiled to herself as she and Jonty walked up to Damien's front door.

But the smile was quickly wiped from her face when

her knock was answered not by Damien but by a woman. A rather striking, glamorous woman dressed in skinny jeans, sky-high stilettos and a figure-hugging top with a plunging neckline that revealed plenty of cleavage between gravity-defying breasts. Who the hell was she?

'Can I help you?' the woman asked as she struck a pose in the doorway, jutting one hip forward as she flicked shiny, sleek hair over her shoulder.

Abi glanced around, thinking she'd perhaps knocked on a neighbour's door by mistake, but this was definitely Damien's house.

'If you're going door to door, selling something, I'm not interested,' the woman said, as Abi stood mute, trying to work out what was going on.

The door was starting to close as Abi regained her senses. 'No, I'm here to see Damien.'

'And you are?'

'I'm Abi, I work with him.' Why had she said that? She wasn't here in a work capacity. She was here because she and Damien had made plans to take Summer out for pizza. And why was anything she did any of this woman's business? But she was too stunned to think of a better retort.

'He's in the shower,' the woman said, as she continued to stand in the doorway. She made no attempt to get out of the way and Abi was certain she was about to shut the door in her face. She certainly didn't appear about to invite her in.

Abi could see Damien over the woman's shoulder. He was dressed in jeans and a shirt but the buttons were open and his feet were bare. He looked half-dressed. His hair was damp from the shower and he was buttoning his shirt as he came towards her, glancing anxiously from her to the woman and back again. He looked surprised to see her, almost as if he'd forgotten about their arrangement, and from the expression on his face she was certain he hadn't been expecting her. But she couldn't blame him. This woman would certainly be more than enough to distract most men. But that still didn't explain who she was.

'Abi! You've met Brooke.'

Abi could feel the blood drain from her face and her hand automatically reached down to pat Jonty's head. She needed the comforting, familiar feel of his warm, soft fur under her icy-cold fingers. She felt as if all the blood was draining from her body.

This stunning, self-assured woman was Brooke!

She looked at her again. She couldn't help but compare herself to the ex-Mrs Moore.

She glowed golden. Her brown hair had been expertly highlighted and straightened and hung in a shiny curtain halfway down her back. Her face was smooth, unlined and her skin was lightly tanned. Abi's trained eye had noted that Brooke's nose was perfect for her face, symmetrical, small and narrow, and her legs were long and slim. Abi felt herself pale in comparison. She felt she was lacking something. She knew she was pretty enough in a young way, she could pass for a teenager some days, and that was the difference. Brooke was all woman. Confident and beautiful and self-satisfied.

'I'll go and finish getting ready,' Brooke said as she shot Abi a smug look that implied she'd won and Abi had no doubt that Damien was the prize.

As she turned on her heel Abi wondered what it was she was getting ready for.

'What is she doing here?' Abi asked, when Damien made no move to invite her inside either.

'I don't know.'

That was a very unsatisfactory answer but Abi let it go for now. 'Are we still going out for pizza?'

Damien shook his head. 'I'm sorry, I can't. I need to find out what Brooke wants.'

So this was how it was going to be, Abi thought. She was going to be shown the door in favour of his ex. She'd wondered where she fitted into the scheme of things, into his life, and now she knew. She could handle coming after his daughter and his career but she didn't want to come after his wife, ex or not. She'd been in that position before and it had ended badly. She wouldn't willingly put herself in that position again.

'Why didn't you call me to cancel?' she asked. She wouldn't have turned up if she'd known. She'd had no desire to meet or even see Brooke. Not without some warning. She wasn't prepared for this.

'I didn't know she was coming. She turned up without warning.'

'What for?'

'I don't know yet. I haven't had time to find out.'

Abi's first response was to panic. She didn't want to confront Damien's past—if that was what Brooke was. What *was* she doing here and what did it mean for Damien and Summer? What did it mean for *her*?

She knew what it meant. She only had to look at Brooke to know.

It meant the fairytale was over. She didn't get to live happily ever after. She didn't get the prince.

'I'll leave you alone, then, to enjoy your evening,' she said. There was no discussion between her fight

and flight responses. Her flight response took over and
she turned around and walked down the path, wanting
to get away before she dissolved into tears, wanting to
run and hide as humiliation crashed over her, shattering
her ridiculous dreams into millions of tiny fragments
that fell around her.

CHAPTER NINE

DAMIEN STOOD AND watched her leave. He was torn, caught between a rock and a hard place. He wanted to go after her, he knew he should go after her, but he didn't trust Brooke. He didn't know why she was there and he had a bad feeling about her reasons.

In the shock accompanying Brooke's unannounced arrival he'd completely forgotten the plans he'd made with Abi. If he'd remembered he would have called her to postpone. The last thing he'd wanted had been for the two of them to meet and the only thing that could make matters worse was if they'd met without him present. He had no idea what had transpired between them but he could only assume Brooke wouldn't have been particularly welcoming. She had a jealous, possessive nature and even though she didn't want him, he had no doubt that she wouldn't want to know that someone else did.

He didn't want Brooke to know about Abi, he didn't want her to start asking questions, so he definitely would have made other arrangements. Not that he could have explained what was going on. He really didn't know what Brooke was doing there but there was sure to be a reason. It would be more than just a visit to see Summer. There was always an ulterior motive as far as his manipulative, scheming ex-wife was concerned. Sure, she did it with charm, using her feminine wiles and acting skills to her advantage, but that didn't change the fact that there was always something to be gained for her. But, at the moment, he hadn't worked out what it was and until he knew the details he wasn't about to leave her alone.

Abi, for all her issues, was far less complicated, far more trusting. There'd be time to sort things out later with her, time to explain, so he let her go. He needed to conserve his energy to deal with Brooke. No doubt there was bound to be some drama or demand, and now it was time to face her music.

Abi had checked her phone a thousand times on Friday night after she'd run from Damien's but he hadn't called once. She'd worked herself up into a fever of indignation, shame and anger and had eventually switched her phone off. She didn't want to be mocked by its silence. She spent the rest of the night imagining all the sorts of things Damien and Brooke might be doing. She knew she was jumping to conclusions but he'd looked so awkward and uncomfortable when she'd appeared on his doorstep, so guilty, that of course her imagination had gone into overdrive.

It appeared she did have a type after all—good-looking, charming men who were only interested in getting her into bed. Did she deliberately choose men who would treat her badly? A psychiatrist would probably tell her it was all connected to issues with her father.

What would Caroline tell her? She knew her psychologist would berate her for thinking unkind thoughts about Damien when he'd done nothing to deserve them, but in Abi's eyes, choosing not to come after her, choosing not to explain, meant that he'd chosen Brooke over her. She couldn't blame him, Brooke was Summer's mother after all, but it hurt that, with everything he'd told her, when the chips were down he hadn't chosen her.

She needed to toughen up, needed to learn from her experiences, her mistakes, and stop being so gullible.

Abi lay in bed all Saturday morning. Her phone showed no missed calls and she couldn't face the thought of getting up and facing the day. She had Jonty and the amber-eyed tiger from the pier for company but neither of them had much to say. Which was fine with her because she didn't feel like talking. She felt like crying.

Jonty seemed to sense her mood. He lay on his stomach on his pillow, looking mournful. He rested his head on his front paws and every now and then he lifted his head as if to check on her before sighing and putting his head down again. She was positive she could read sympathy in his brown eyes but perhaps he was just bored and waiting patiently for a walk.

Eventually she gave in and got out of bed and pulled on her exercise gear. Last night she'd decided she needed to toughen up, she wasn't going to fall apart because a man had changed his mind.

Jonty raced down the stairs eagerly the moment Abi tied the laces of her sneakers, and to make up for her lazy, self-indulgent morning she intended to take him for a long walk.

It was getting dark as she turned into her driveway later and she was startled to find a man leaning against her garage door. She panicked briefly until she recognised him.

Tall and dark, lean and gorgeous.

Damien.

Her heart rate continued to accelerate at the sight of him. 'What are you doing here?'

'I wanted to see you. I need to talk to you and you didn't answer your phone.'

She'd left her phone behind for the walk. There hadn't seemed to be any point in carrying a phone that never rang. 'I thought you were busy with your wife and family.'

'Ex-wife,' he corrected. 'Have you got a minute? I need your advice.'

He looked so desperate it was almost impossible to stay mad at him. Her heart wasn't built to resist him. 'You'd better come in,' she sighed.

She made coffee and let Damien talk while she listened.

'I'm sorry I didn't let you know Brooke was in town. She honestly just appeared without warning. It took me by surprise and with Brooke the surprises are generally not pleasant. This time was no exception.'

'What is she doing here?' Abi asked, although what she really wanted to ask was, *Where did she stay last night and what have you been doing?*

'She's been offered a permanent role in the sitcom. She came to tell me she's staying in New York.'

'What does that mean for you and Summer?' With one question Abi had got to the heart of the problem.

'I don't know. That's what I wanted to talk to you about. I need to work out what my options are but I need to base my decisions on what is best for Summer. She is my priority and you are the person who knows us best. I need your opinion. I've always said I would do what's best for Summer but it turns out I don't know what that is,' he admitted. 'Is keeping her away from her mother the best thing? Or should I move to New York?'

Abi didn't want to answer that question. She knew she couldn't answer it without bias. She knew Damien had moved to LA because of Brooke and she'd been afraid that he would move again to keep his family together, but surely there had to come a time where he wouldn't be manipulated by Brooke?

Abi knew she was thinking of her own interests as well when she answered but did that matter when she also believed she was thinking of what was best for Summer too? 'Does Summer want to go?'

'No.' He shook his head and continued, 'But she is five, she doesn't get to decide.'

'Has Brooke asked for Summer to go to New York?'

'No.'

'Then there's absolutely nothing wrong with keeping Summer with you. Brooke has made no secret of the fact she doesn't want a child. You're not obliged to send Summer or to move you both. Let Summer visit her in New York. Better yet, make Brooke come here.'

'We'll have to come to some sort of official agreement if we're living on opposite sides of the country. I'm not sure if the courts will give me sole custody.'

'Well, then, you'll just have to find out about all the hoops you'll need to jump through to keep her and be prepared to start jumping. Child care will be the big thing but I imagine Brooke's hours are as inconsistent as yours so as long as you make good arrangements for that you might be okay. You can afford child care but you'll need something more permanent than sending Summer to Irma's. After-school care only covers you for so long. It's not a bad option, it gives Summer some interaction with other kids, but perhaps it's not ideal every day. You'll need a nanny or some organised care.'

'Do you think I can manage on my own? Do you think that's fair to Summer?'

'Trust me, having one parent who loves her and puts her first is all she will need.' Abi knew that she was speaking the truth this time, she had plenty of experience in that department. 'You're doing a fabulous job with her. You can do this.'

She knew she should have sent him on his way when she'd discovered him on her doorstep but she hadn't been able to resist him. He still looked a bit overwhelmed by the situation but Abi knew he would work it out. He was an intelligent, sensible man and she hoped he made an intelligent, sensible decision.

She could forgive him for the past twenty-four hours, she could forgive him for putting Summer first. She could give him forgiveness but what did she get?

She wasn't sure yet.

She was on tenterhooks for the next few days, waiting to hear what his decision was, but everything was quiet.

Every time there was a knock on her office door she found herself hoping that it would be Damien, bringing her the news she was desperate to hear, but each time she was disappointed.

And this latest interruption was no exception. There was a knock on the door and it opened to reveal Brooke. She was still in sky-high stilettos but she'd swapped the skinny jeans for a figure-hugging dress.

'I'm sorry,' she said. 'I thought this was Damien's office. I'm meeting him for lunch.'

Brooke was the last person Abi wanted to see. She'd been hoping for the news that Brooke had returned to New York but clearly that wasn't the case. 'He's next door,' Abi said, hoping to move her on, but instead she stepped into the room.

From her deliberate action and calm and measured manner Abi suspected she hadn't mixed up the offices at all. She suspected that Brooke had orchestrated this meeting but what she wanted to know was why. Had she won the battle over Damien? The battle Abi hadn't even realised they were having?

She wasn't kept in suspense for long.

'Seeing as you're so close to Damien and Summer, I expect you've heard the news?' Brooke said as she arched one finely plucked and expertly made-up eyebrow.

'What news?' Abi said, wishing as the words came out of her mouth that she'd kept quiet. She didn't want to know any news that Brooke might want to impart. A sixth sense told her it could only mean bad news for her.

'Damien and I are reconciling. He's moving to New York.'

Abi's stomach lurched. Too late she wished she'd pretended to be busy and sent Brooke on her way. Each word had felt like a punch she would never recover from. She felt ridiculous, naive, used and stupid. She'd given him her advice and her body. He'd asked her for advice but he hadn't listened. She'd given herself to him but he hadn't been honest with her. All she wanted was honesty.

She liked to think she was clever but she obviously

wasn't smart. Not worldly-wise. She was pathetic. When would she learn?

'No, I hadn't heard that.' She wondered if Brooke was expecting her to congratulate her. If she was, she was going to be disappointed. Abi summoned up all her reserves and said, 'If you'll excuse me, I have patients to see. You'll find Damien next door.' She forced the words out and prayed that Brooke would go away and leave her alone.

She sank into her chair and watched Brooke leave, knowing she couldn't compete. All she'd wanted was for Damien to find her attractive, but now that she'd met Brooke she realised there was no way she could measure up if Brooke was the type of woman he desired. Abi was far too different.

She put her head in her hands and let the tears flow. She was a fool. When would she learn?

'Abi? Is everything okay?'

She looked up at the sound of her name to find Mila in her doorway.

'What's happened?'

Abi reached for a tissue and wiped her eyes. The tissue came away streaked with mascara.

'It's nothing,' she said, as she threw the tissue in the trash.

Mila closed the office door. Was nobody going to leave her alone today? She wanted to lick her wounds in private but that wasn't being terribly professional. Mila must have come to see her about Dylan. She hoped everything was all right.

'Did you need to see me?'

'I was in the clinic so I thought I'd just give you an

update on Dylan but that can wait. Why don't you tell me what's wrong?'

'It's nothing, really. I just got some news that's upset me but I'll be fine. I just need a moment to get my head together.'

'Is it Damien?'

'Why do you say that?'

'At our age it's always men,' she said, as she came and sat by Abi's desk. 'What's he done?'

'He hasn't done anything yet but I think he's about to break my heart.' She sniffed and reached for another tissue. 'It's my own fault. Neither of us were ready for a proper relationship. I got ahead of myself.'

'What do you mean?'

'I had all these romantic notions but it seems he didn't share them.' They may not have talked about it but she had been building a fantasy in her head. A happily-ever-after where she and Damien got to spend the rest of their lives together, along with Summer and children of their own. It was a fantasy that had taken hold on the day they'd spent at the pier and she didn't want to let it go. But it seemed she might have to. 'Apparently he's planning on moving to New York with his ex-wife.'

'Really? He's just told you this?'

Abi shook her head. 'His ex has just paid me a visit. She told me.'

'And you believe her?'

'Why would she lie to me?'

'I don't know but I take it you don't want to let him go?'

'No.'

'Does he know how you feel?'

'No.' Abi loved him but she was terrified of telling him. She was terrified that it would jinx everything, even though it seemed that everything was already ruined. She wasn't about to humiliate herself further by telling him how she felt. 'I can't tell him I've fallen in love with him. I couldn't bear to hear that he doesn't love me.'

'So you're prepared to give him up?'

'No.'

'Then you have to tell him how you feel. You have to take the chance that his ex was lying to you. You have to take the chance that he feels the same way you do. You can't let him go without questions. You'll always wonder "what if." Trust me, I'm speaking from experience.'

'You've had your heart broken?'

Mia nodded. 'In the worst possible way.'

'Was it James?' Abi knew instinctively that it was. It would explain all that tension she had felt between the two of them.

Mila nodded again. 'James left me standing at the altar without an explanation and I have never found out why.'

'You didn't ask?'

'I didn't want to know at first but not knowing has stopped me from moving on.'

'Why don't you take your own advice? Why don't you ask him now?'

'It's too late. There is no point in raking up the past. But it's not too late for you. Don't let him go without a fight. Don't let him go without an explanation. You need to hear it from Damien's lips.'

Mila was right. Abi felt betrayed and she deserved some answers. She deserved some honesty.

She waited until the end of the day to confront him. She didn't want to run into Brooke again and she definitely didn't want to run into Damien and Brooke together.

'Can I speak to you?' she asked, as she stepped into his office and closed the door. 'I bumped into Brooke today. She told me you are getting back together.' Abi didn't give him an opportunity to speak. She needed to keep going, she needed to get her feelings out in the open before she lost her nerve. She paced up and down in front of his desk. 'How can you be having that conversation with her and sleeping with me at the same time? You know how Mark's lies and deception hurt me, you know what that did to me, and yet you've been sleeping with me and making plans with your wife behind my back.'

'Ex-wife. She's my *ex*-wife.' Damien stood up and ushered Abi to a chair.

'How could you do that to me? Do I matter so little?'

'Abi, listen to me. I haven't done anything that you're accusing me of. When did you speak to Brooke?'

'She came into my office before she met you for lunch.'

He frowned. 'We didn't have lunch. I haven't seen her today.'

'Do you think I'm making this up?' Abi wasn't sure who to believe, Damien or Brooke. She desperately wanted to believe Damien but she didn't know if she should.

'Of course I don't.'

'She was here,' Abi insisted.

'But she wasn't here to see me. And we are *not* getting back together.'

'You're not?'

'No. Why would you think that?'

'You have moved before for Summer. You told me you moved here from San Francisco for that very reason. I thought you might have decided that it was best for Summer.'

'I did it once before and it was a mistake. But do you think I would make this decision and not tell you myself?'

'Brooke was very convincing.'

'I don't doubt that, she's a very good actress,' he said as he sat down opposite Abi. 'She's fooled me more than once. When I met her she was a drama student sporting a black eye. She told me she and another student had collided heads when they'd been rehearsing a fight scene. Then later she told me that it was actually from her boyfriend, that he'd hit her. She'd worked out by then that I had protective instincts. She told me he was abusing her and of course I believed her and came to her rescue.

'The truth was that she saw me as someone who would be able to provide her with financial security while she pursued her career. I was a better bet than the actor she was dating plus I would be able to keep her looking good. Brooke is self-centred and narcissistic. Everything is about her. She doesn't want to be a wife and mother, she wants to be a successful actress, and she has used me to get herself there.'

'I thought you might not be able to resist Brooke. After seeing her, I couldn't blame you.'

'You're kidding, aren't you? What is under the surface is far more important. Believe me when I tell you there is absolutely nothing attractive about her.'

'Why was she here today if it wasn't to see you?'

'She came to see James for some minor cosmetic surgery.'

'James? Not you?'

Damien shook his head. 'Not me. I won't perform any more procedures on her.'

'You've done some in the past?'

He nodded. 'She's had her nose narrowed,' he said, and Abi felt a twinge of satisfaction. She'd been sure Brooke's nose was too perfect to be natural. 'She's also had her lips enlarged and after she had Summer she wanted her breasts reshaped and enlarged. I did all that but I refused to do any more surgery once Summer turned three.'

'Why?'

'Summer was old enough then to be aware of changes to Brooke's appearance. I didn't want her asking why her mother was always changing her looks. I didn't want her asking why *I* was changing Brooke's appearance. Hollywood is a superficial place, I didn't want to perpetuate the idea of physical beauty being the pinnacle of success to my own daughter, and that was the danger if I continued to operate on her mother. So I stopped.'

'But why would she lie to me? What was the point?'

'Think of it from her point of view. It's always about Brooke. She wants to be the centre of attention. Summer has been talking about you and Brooke doesn't want her attention on anyone else. She doesn't want us but she craves attention. You have to trust me when I say Brooke is not part of my life. I moved on a long time ago.'

'But that's the point,' Abi argued. 'You might think you've moved on but she will always be part of your life because of Summer. You can't cut her out but you need to decide how you want this to work. I can't invest myself in us until you've worked out what you want. I want honesty and I'm not prepared to play Brooke's games.' She wasn't sure she could handle her games or the additional stress.

Damien reached for Abi's hands and pulled her out of the chair. He wrapped her in his arms as he said, 'I have never lied to you and I promise I will work this out. I don't want you to worry about Brooke. Leave her to me.'

Abi relaxed slightly but she doubted it was going to be as easy to deal with Brooke as he would have her believe. But she would give him some time and space to sort things out. She had to make sure he had done that before she could invest in the relationship; she had to be able to trust him.

Damien grabbed his car keys and headed for the door. He had some letters to dictate but he'd have to come back later and finish those—there were things that couldn't wait. He was furious but he knew how to handle Brooke. She would have an agenda and he'd bet his last dollar that he knew what it was.

Brooke was lying on the sofa with an icepack on her forehead—the aftermath of her visit to James—when Damien got home, but at least she had collected Summer from school. He sent Summer to her room while he spoke to Brooke. He was still furious and he didn't want Summer to hear this conversation.

'What did you think you were doing at the clinic?'

Brooke lifted the ice pack from her forehead but didn't sit up. Her unlined face was a picture of innocence as she asked. 'What are you talking about?'

'Did you think Abi wouldn't tell me what you said? What game are you playing?'

'It's not a game. I want Summer with me and I didn't think you'd let her go without you. Therefore, that means you will move to New York.'

'I am not moving to New York and neither is our daughter.' He knew she was just trying to make him angry so he would give her what she really wanted. He just had to find out what that was. 'You don't want us. You definitely don't want me. I don't think you ever did. Tell me what you really want. You know I'll give it to you.'

He suddenly realised what she was after. Money and fame. It shouldn't surprise him. That was always what it was about with Brooke. Nothing had changed. She wanted Summer with her so that Damien would fund her lifestyle. Two could play that game. 'I won't give you Summer. She is staying with me but she can visit. If you agree that Summer can stay here, I am prepared to help you with your rent. I want you to have somewhere nice when Summer comes to stay.'

He took a chance that appealing to Brooke's avaricious nature would pay off. They would need to make some arrangements but he would do whatever was needed to ensure that Brooke didn't cause more complications, and then he could work out how to fix things with Abi.

CHAPTER TEN

THREE DAYS LATER Abi pulled her car to the kerb behind a moving truck that was parked in front of Damien's house. She locked her car and dodged around dozens of packing boxes that were stacked on the pavement. The boxes were all marked 'New York City'. Abi's heart plummeted and she thought she was going to be sick.

Damien had asked her to call past after work. Had he made his decision? Had he been lying to her all along? Was he taking Summer and moving to New York?

Two men were loading the boxes into the truck. Abi stopped when she noticed Brooke's name on one. She glanced at the other boxes. They were all addressed to Brooke.

She walked through the open front door.

Summer was playing on the floor but jumped up when she walked in. 'Abi, I haven't seen you for ages.'

Abi had been avoiding everyone, not just Damien. She'd avoided Mila, Irma and George and even Summer.

Summer ran to Abi and hugged her, wrapping her arms around Abi's legs. She picked her up to hug her properly and let her tuck her warm little body against her side. She felt so soft and sweet and innocent. Abi's eyes brimmed with tears as she gently put the little girl down. She had missed Summer almost as much as she'd missed Damien.

And thinking of the devil, there he was in all his dark handsomeness. Dressed casually in jeans that hugged his thighs and a black sweater that made his eyes gleam, he crossed the room and reached for her. She knew he was going to kiss her but she wasn't sure if she was ready for that. She needed to know the state of play. When she folded her arms protectively across her chest, he backed away.

More packing boxes lined the hallway and were stacked against the wall of the lounge. 'What's going on?' she asked.

'Thank you for coming. I wanted you to see this,' Damien said, as he gestured at more boxes that lined the passageway and led her out of the lounge and into the kitchen, out of earshot of Summer. 'These are all Brooke's things,' he said, as they walked through the house. 'She is officially out of here.'

'She's gone?'

'She left this morning.' He pulled a key from the pocket of his jeans and held it up triumphantly. 'She's even returned her key.'

'How did that happen?'

'I made her an offer she couldn't refuse.'

'What was it?'

'I will contribute to her rent in New York to make sure that she has somewhere decent to live when Summer visits.'

'Visits? Does that mean you're staying here?'

Damien grinned. 'It does. Brooke gets what she's wanted all along—financial security and the freedom to follow her dream—and hopefully that means that we can all get what we want.'

'We?'

'You were right. Brooke will always be a part of my life because of Summer, but that's all. There is nothing between us, there hasn't been for a long time, and if you'll let me I want to make it up to you.' He took hold of her hand and pressed his house key into her palm before closing her fist and wrapping his hand around hers. 'I want you to have this key.'

The sharp edges of the key dug into her palm. It was uncomfortable and didn't feel right. She wasn't sure about this. She wanted to be a part of Damien's life, of Summer's life, but she wasn't sure if they were thinking of it in the same vein.

She opened her palm and looked at the key. 'Can I think about it?' she asked.

'That wasn't the answer I was hoping for.'

It wasn't the offer Abi had been hoping for either but she didn't tell him that. She wasn't about to put words into his mouth. This was a start but it wasn't enough. It told her that Brooke was as good as gone but she didn't know where that left her.

Abi didn't want a key to the castle—she wanted the key to the prince's heart. What she felt for Damien and Summer was real. She didn't want a casual relationship, she didn't want a key so she could come and go. She wanted it all; she wanted the fairytale.

Abi remembered her discussion with Mila. She had to talk about her feelings. She needed to know exactly what he wanted from her and she had to tell him how she felt. She had to know she'd given everything she had to Damien and to pursuing her dream. At least then if she failed she'd know she'd done everything possible.

'I'm not sure I want a key to your house,' she said, and she lifted the key out of her palm and returned it to him. 'I appreciate the gesture but I want to be more than someone who leaves a toothbrush in your bathroom and stays over for the weekend. I have a different vision.'

Damien took the key but it sat heavy in his hand, just like his heart sat heavy in his chest.

He hadn't expected his offer to be rejected but he wasn't prepared to let go of his dream. He had a vision too, a vision of his future, and Abi was part of that. There was no way he was going to risk losing her.

'This is more than a key to my house,' he explained. 'This is a key to *our* house.'

'Our house?'

He nodded. 'You told me to work out what I wanted. I know exactly what I want. I want to start a new life with you. This is your key to our house. I want you to move in with us.'

'You want me to move in?'

'I want to show you that I am serious about us, that I'm committed to you. I'm giving you this key because I want you in my life. This isn't a spur-of-the-moment decision. My life is complete when you are there and I want to keep you in it. I've fallen in love with you and I want to see where this will lead.'

'You love me?' Abi was watching him solemnly but at least she was listening.

'I do. This key is just the beginning. I wasn't much good at being married,' he continued. 'I'm not sure if I know how to have a good marriage, a happy one, and I wasn't prepared to ever give it another shot, but you make me want to consider it and I'm hoping you will consider it too. I want you to be part of my life and of Summer's. I want you to feel safe with us, I want you to trust me. I'll give you all the time you need but I want you here. With us.' He held the key between his thumb and forefinger, offering it to her again. 'I love you, Abi. Please say you'll take a chance on me.'

She smiled and her amber eyes shone with fire as she reached out and took the key from his fingers. 'I will,' she said.

'You will?'

'Yes,' she answered him with a smile. 'I want this too. I want a future with you and Summer, a chance to build a life together, to be a family. I want *you*.' Abi leant in and kissed him. 'I love you too.'

The kiss was soft and tender. It wasn't crazy with desire, it was gentle with love, and it released his trapped and heavy heart. He took her in his arms as his heart soared in his chest and filled with love.

'Welcome home,' he said.

* * * * *

Look out for the next story in the fabulous
THE HOLLYWOOD HILLS CLINIC *series:*
TEMPTED BY HOLLYWOOD'S TOP DOC
by Louisa George.

MILLS & BOON®
Hardback – April 2016

ROMANCE

The Sicilian's Stolen Son	Lynne Graham
Seduced into Her Boss's Service	Cathy Williams
The Billionaire's Defiant Acquisition	Sharon Kendrick
One Night to Wedding Vows	Kim Lawrence
Engaged to Her Ravensdale Enemy	Melanie Milburne
A Diamond Deal with the Greek	Maya Blake
Inherited by Ferranti	Kate Hewitt
The Secret to Marrying Marchesi	Amanda Cinelli
The Billionaire's Baby Swap	Rebecca Winters
The Wedding Planner's Big Day	Cara Colter
Holiday with the Best Man	Kate Hardy
Tempted by Her Tycoon Boss	Jennie Adams
Seduced by the Heart Surgeon	Carol Marinelli
Falling for the Single Dad	Emily Forbes
The Fling That Changed Everything	Alison Roberts
A Child to Open Their Hearts	Marion Lennox
The Greek Doctor's Secret Son	Jennifer Taylor
Caught in a Storm of Passion	Lucy Ryder
Take Me, Cowboy	Maisey Yates
His Baby Agenda	Katherine Garbera

MILLS & BOON®
Large Print – April 2016

ROMANCE

The Price of His Redemption	Carol Marinelli
Back in the Brazilian's Bed	Susan Stephens
The Innocent's Sinful Craving	Sara Craven
Brunetti's Secret Son	Maya Blake
Talos Claims His Virgin	Michelle Smart
Destined for the Desert King	Kate Walker
Ravensdale's Defiant Captive	Melanie Milburne
The Best Man & The Wedding Planner	Teresa Carpenter
Proposal at the Winter Ball	Jessica Gilmore
Bodyguard...to Bridegroom?	Nikki Logan
Christmas Kisses with Her Boss	Nina Milne

HISTORICAL

His Christmas Countess	Louise Allen
The Captain's Christmas Bride	Annie Burrows
Lord Lansbury's Christmas Wedding	Helen Dickson
Warrior of Fire	Michelle Willingham
Lady Rowena's Ruin	Carol Townend

MEDICAL

The Baby of Their Dreams	Carol Marinelli
Falling for Her Reluctant Sheikh	Amalie Berlin
Hot-Shot Doc, Secret Dad	Lynne Marshall
Father for Her Newborn Baby	Lynne Marshall
His Little Christmas Miracle	Emily Forbes
Safe in the Surgeon's Arms	Molly Evans

MILLS & BOON®
Hardback – May 2016

ROMANCE

Morelli's Mistress	Anne Mather
A Tycoon to Be Reckoned With	Julia James
Billionaire Without a Past	Carol Marinelli
The Shock Cassano Baby	Andie Brock
The Most Scandalous Ravensdale	Melanie Milburne
The Sheikh's Last Mistress	Rachael Thomas
Claiming the Royal Innocent	Jennifer Hayward
Kept at the Argentine's Command	Lucy Ellis
The Billionaire Who Saw Her Beauty	Rebecca Winters
In the Boss's Castle	Jessica Gilmore
One Week with the French Tycoon	Christy McKellen
Rafael's Contract Bride	Nina Milne
Tempted by Hollywood's Top Doc	Louisa George
Perfect Rivals...	Amy Ruttan
English Rose in the Outback	Lucy Clark
A Family for Chloe	Lucy Clark
The Doctor's Baby Secret	Scarlet Wilson
Married for the Boss's Baby	Susan Carlisle
Twins for the Texan	Charlene Sands
Secret Baby Scandal	Joanne Rock

MILLS & BOON®
Large Print – May 2016

ROMANCE

HISTORICAL

MEDICAL

MILLS & BOON®

Why shop at millsandboon.co.uk?

Each year, thousands of romance readers find their perfect read at millsandboon.co.uk. That's because we're passionate about bringing you the very best romantic fiction. Here are some of the advantages of shopping at www.millsandboon.co.uk:

* **Get new books first**—you'll be able to buy your favourite books one month before they hit the shops

* **Get exclusive discounts**—you'll also be able to buy our specially created monthly collections, with up to 50% off the RRP

* **Find your favourite authors**—latest news, interviews and new releases for all your favourite authors and series on our website, plus ideas for what to try next

* **Join in**—once you've bought your favourite books, don't forget to register with us to rate, review and join in the discussions

Visit **www.millsandboon.co.uk**
for all this and more today!